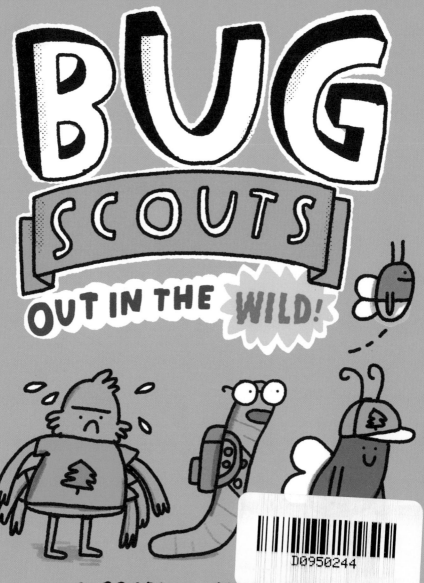

BUG SCOUTS

OUT IN THE WILD!

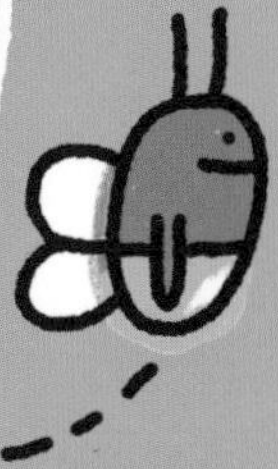

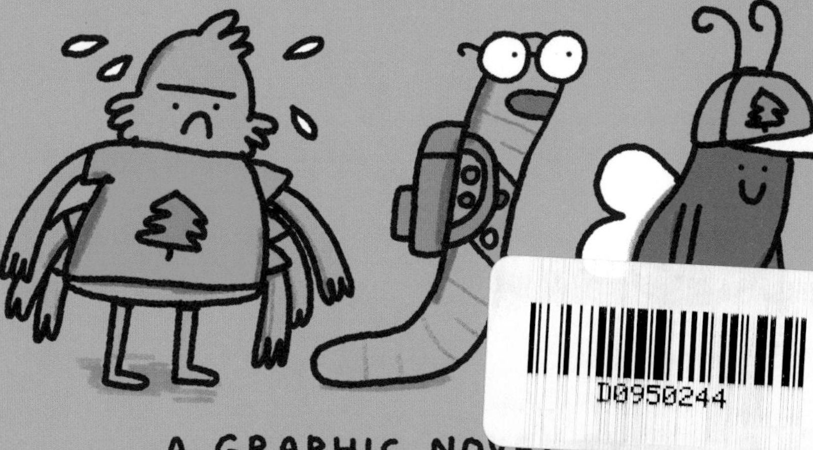

A GRAPHIC NOVEL BY

MIKE LOWERY

graphix
An Imprint of
SCHOLASTIC

Dedicated to Abby
(who is definitely not a worm)
and Noah
(who is probably not a bug of any sort)

Library of Congress Cataloging-in-Publication Data Available

ISBN 978-1-338-72633-6 (hardcover)
ISBN 978-1-338-72632-9 (paperback)

10 9 8 7 6 5 4 3 2 1   22 23 24 25 26

Printed in China   62
First edition, May 2022

Edited by Liza Baker and Rachel Matson
Book design by Doan Buu
Creative Director: Phil Falco
Publisher: David Saylor

CONTENTS

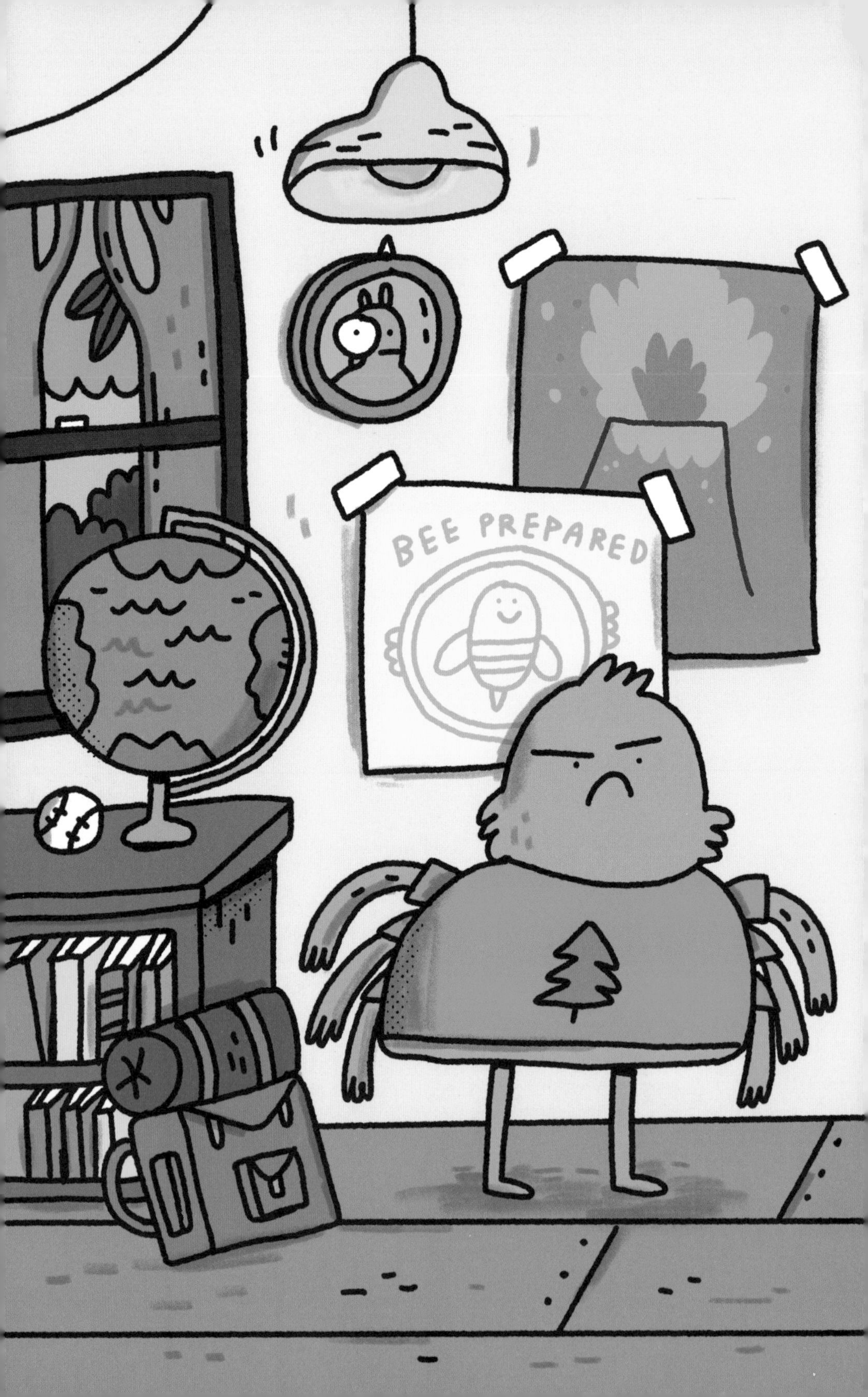
BEE PREPARED

CHAPTER 1

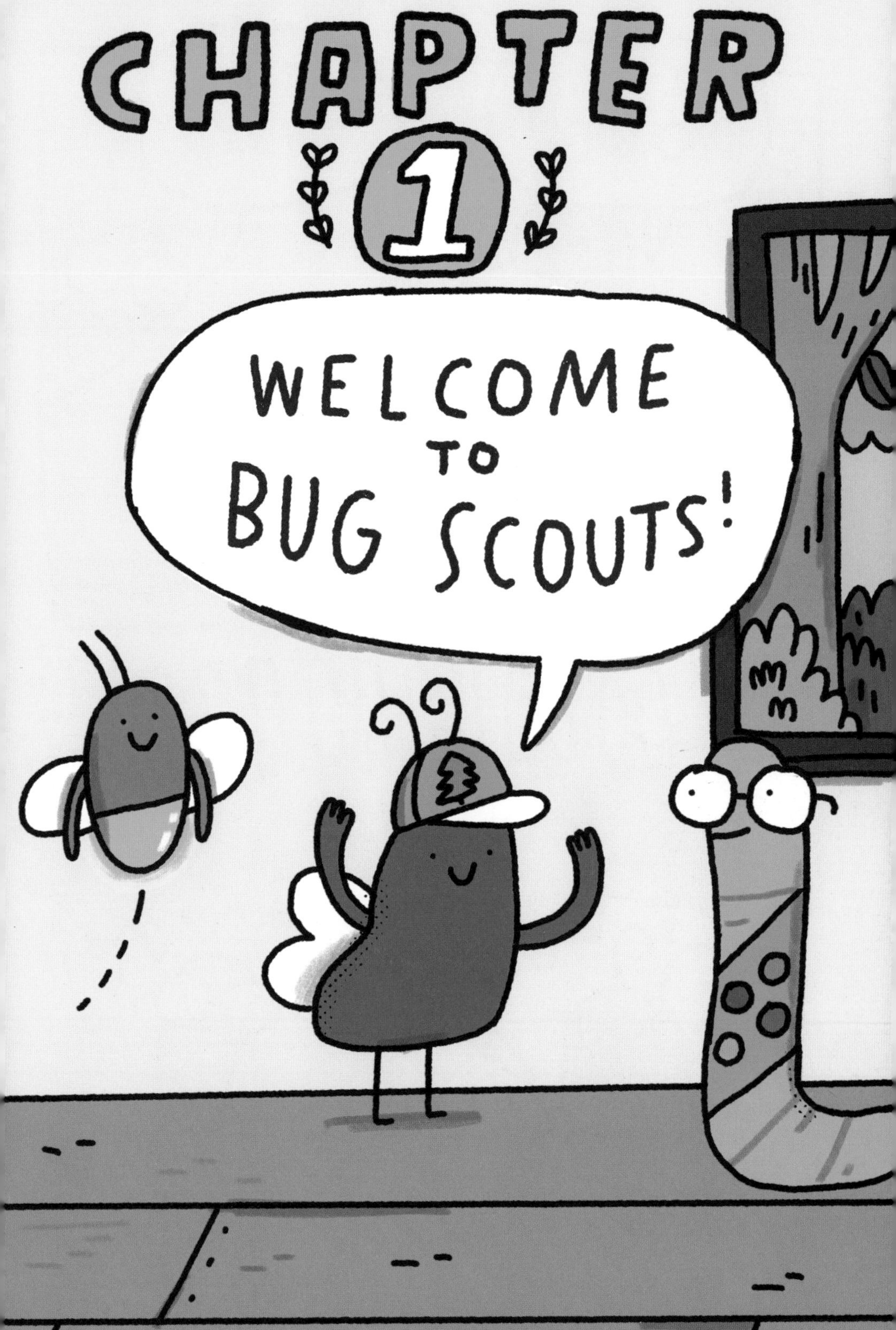
WELCOME TO BUG SCOUTS!

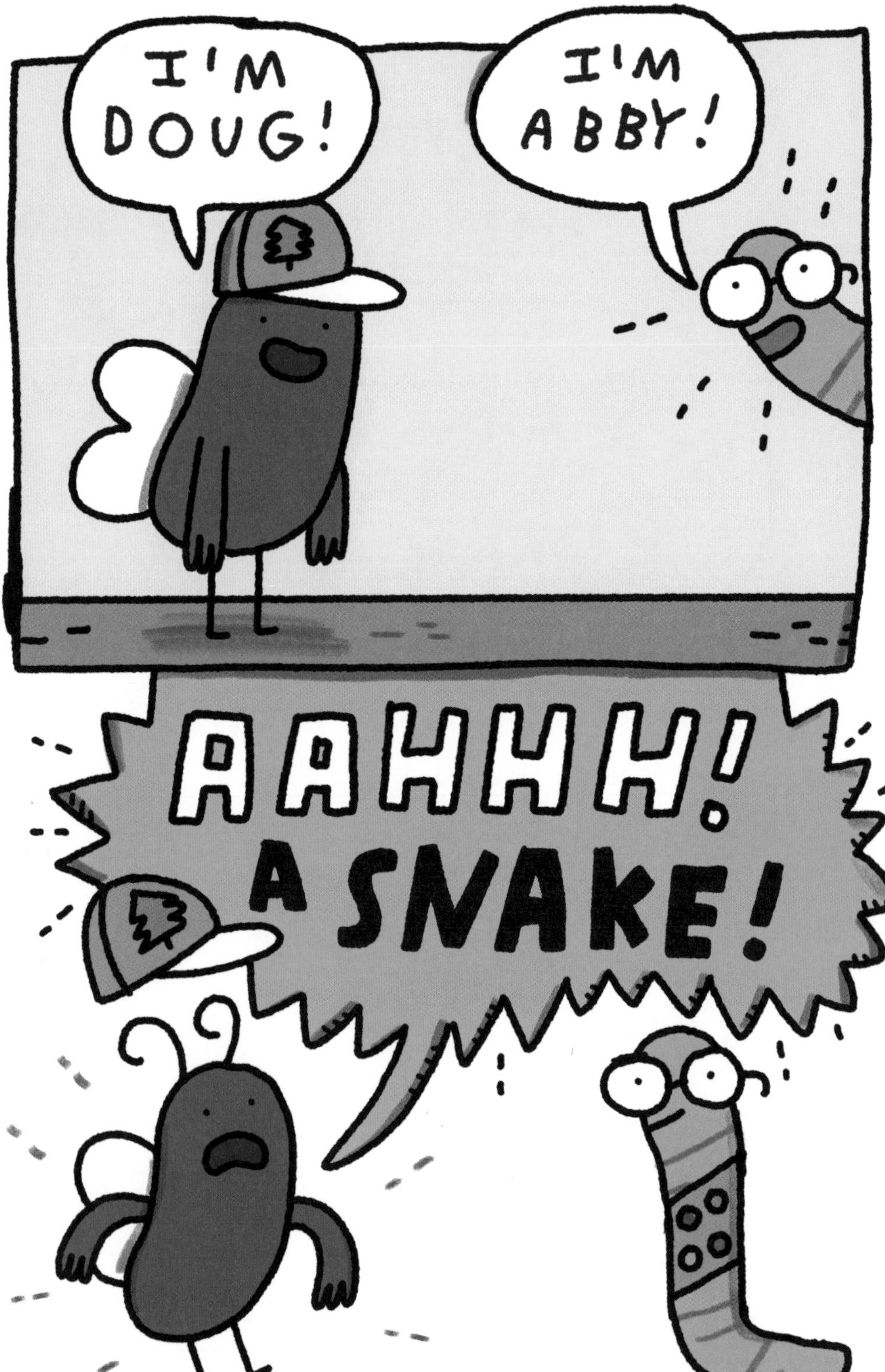
I'M DOUG!
I'M ABBY!
AAHHH! A SNAKE!

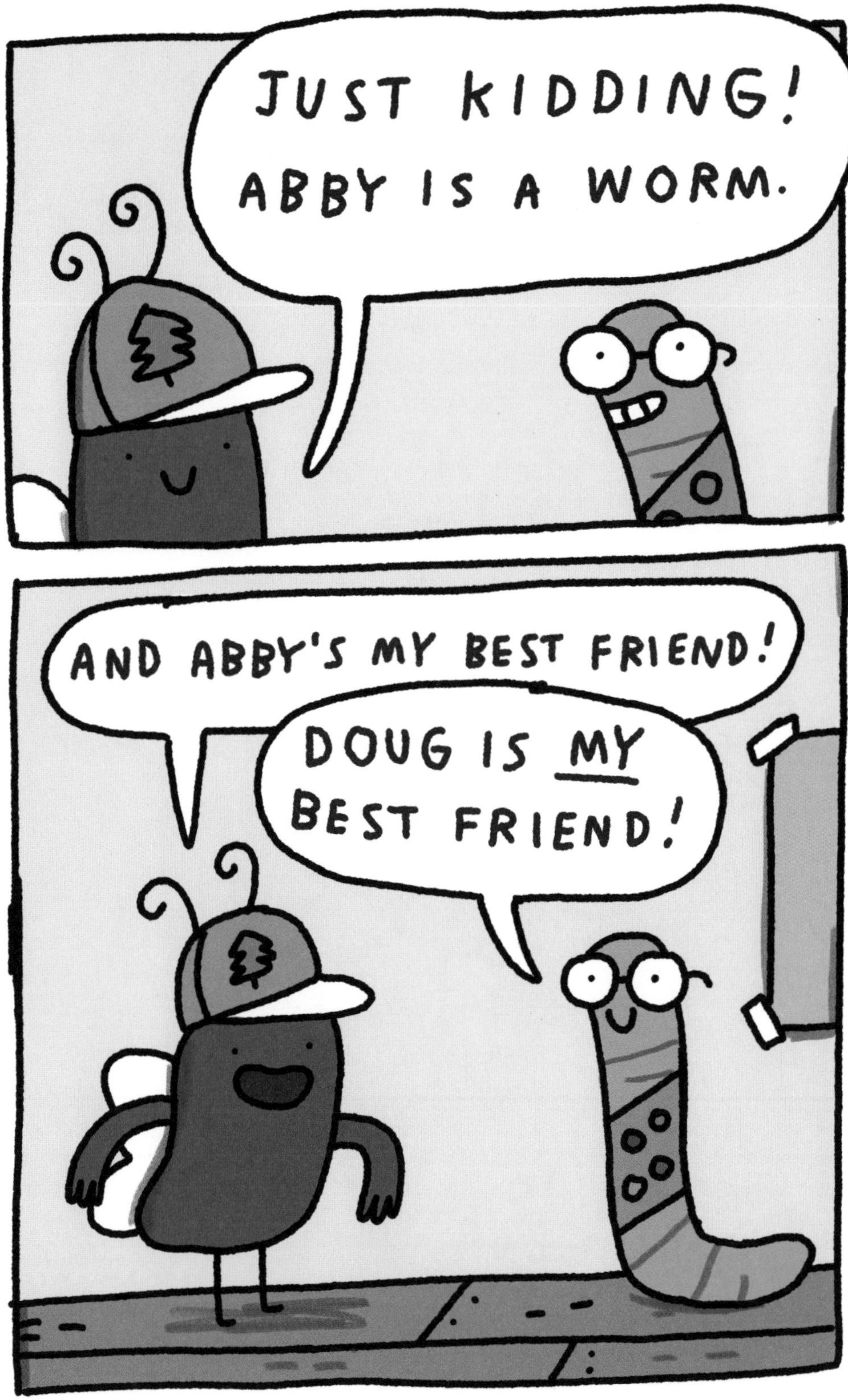
JUST KIDDING! ABBY IS A WORM.
AND ABBY'S MY BEST FRIEND!
DOUG IS MY BEST FRIEND!

DOUG

(SOME KIND OF BUG)

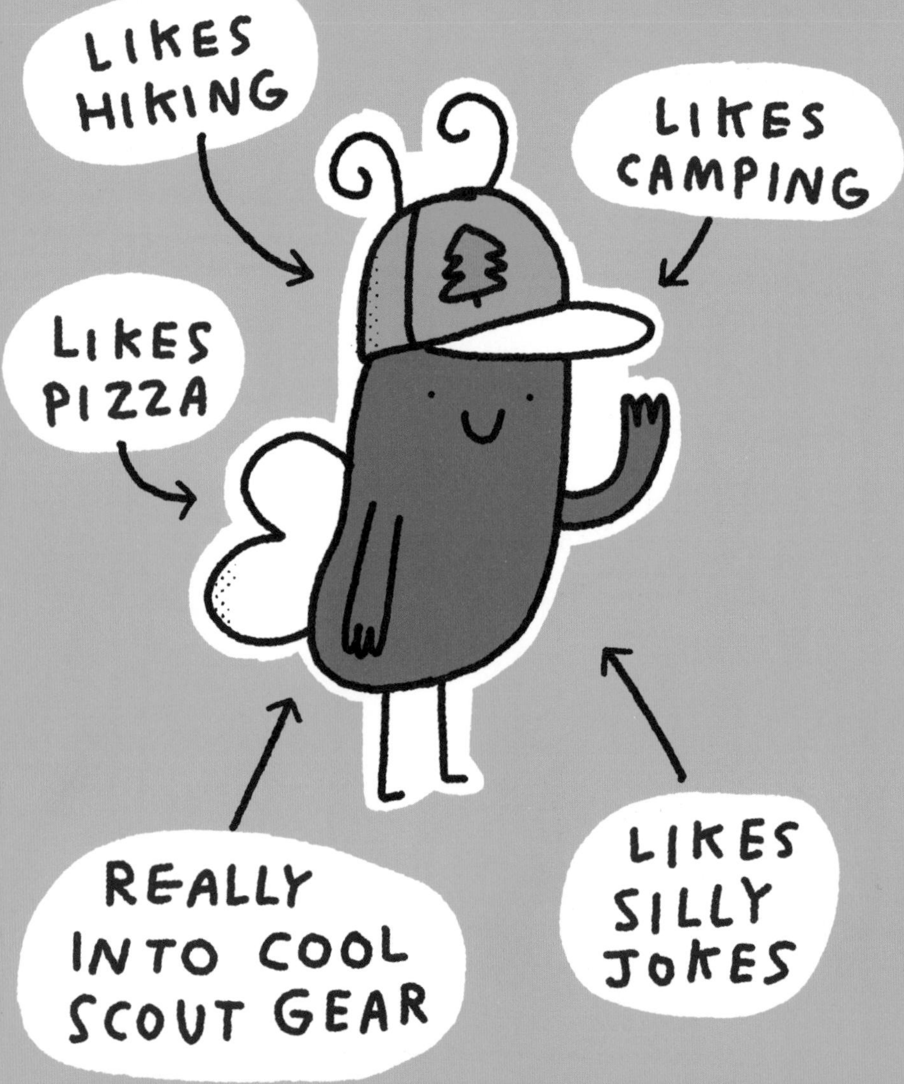
LIKES HIKING
LIKES CAMPING
LIKES PIZZA
REALLY INTO COOL SCOUT GEAR
LIKES SILLY JOKES

SCIENTIFIC NAME:
"SOMEKINDICUS BUGICUS"

ABBY

(WORM)

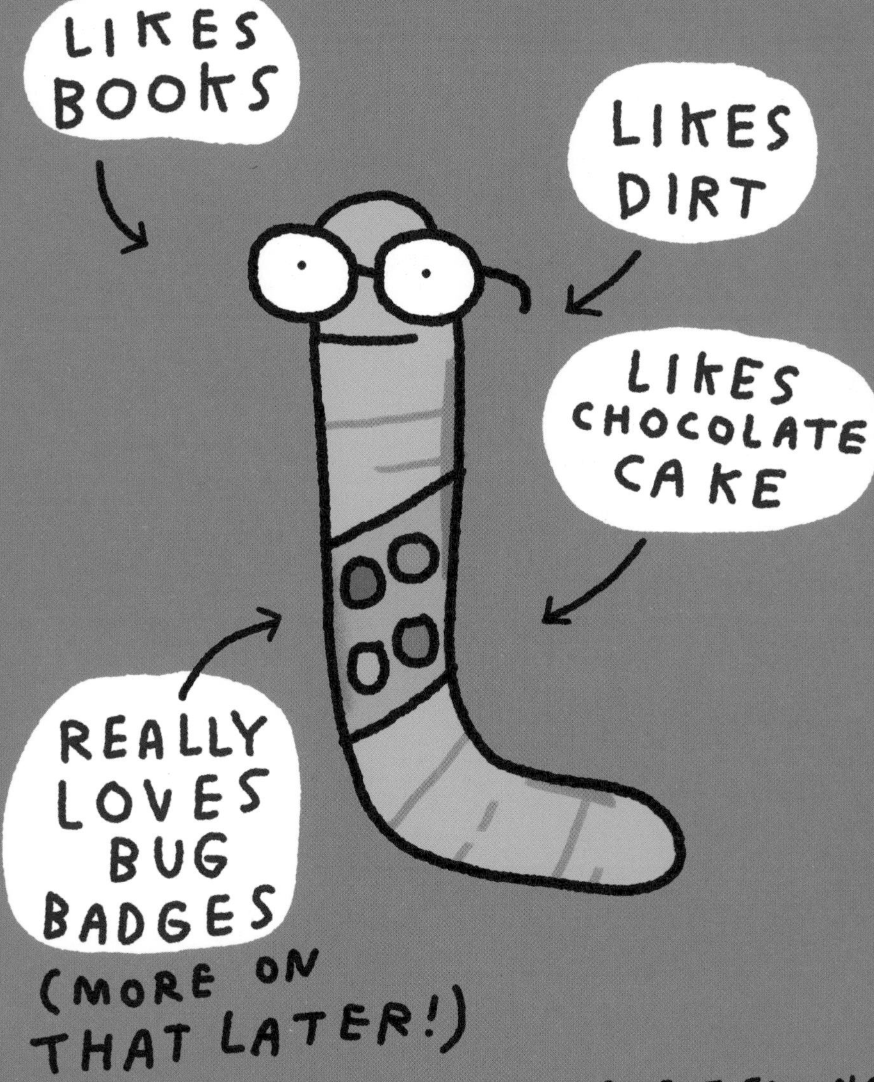

SCIENTIFIC NAME:
"LUMBRICUS TERRESTRIS"

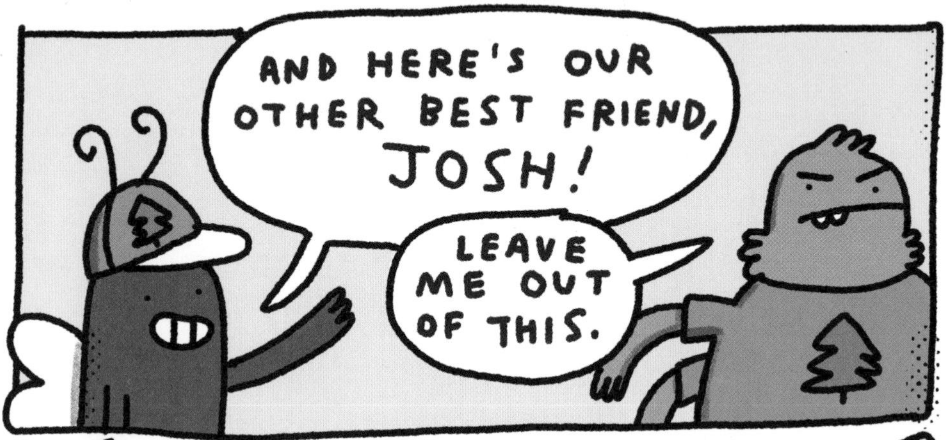
AND HERE'S OUR OTHER BEST FRIEND, JOSH!
LEAVE ME OUT OF THIS.

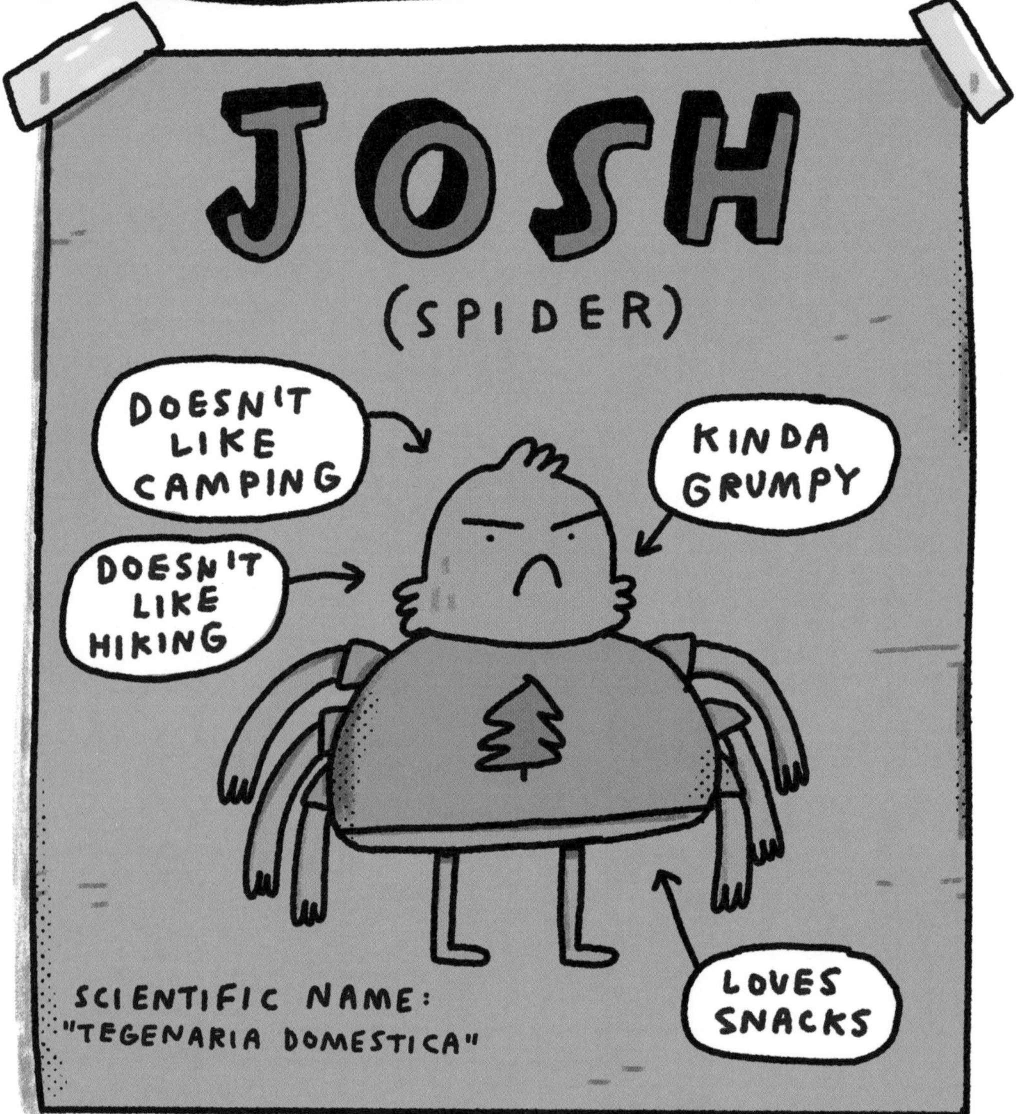
JOSH
(SPIDER)
DOESN'T LIKE CAMPING
KINDA GRUMPY
DOESN'T LIKE HIKING
LOVES SNACKS
SCIENTIFIC NAME: "TEGENARIA DOMESTICA"

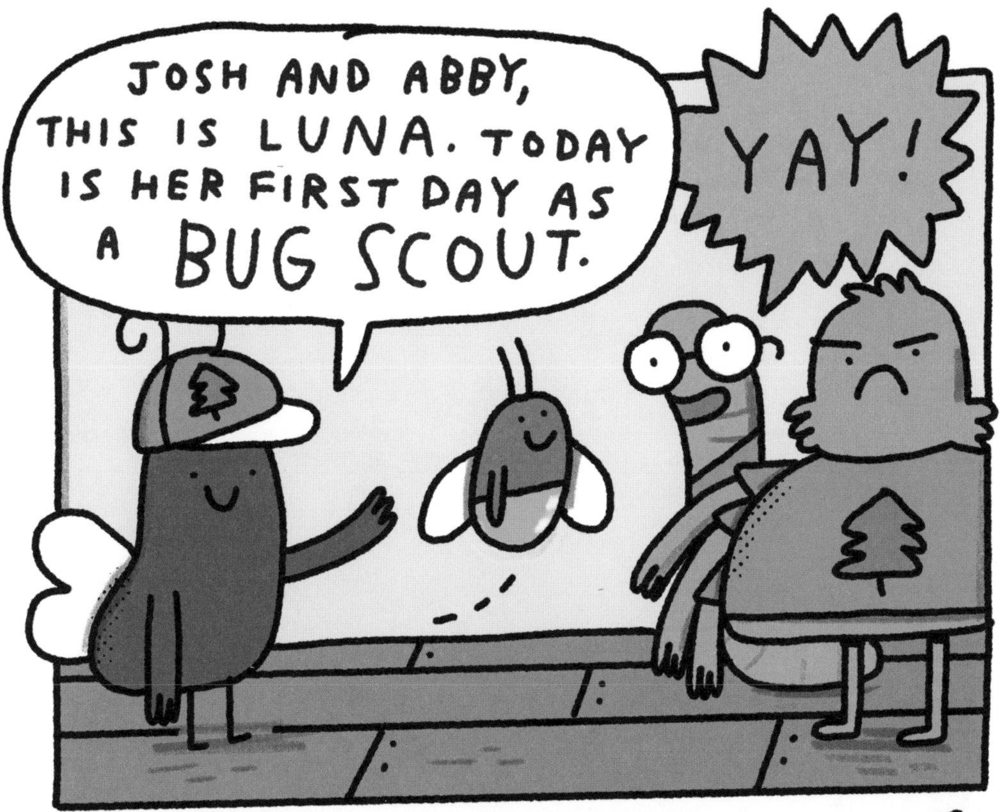
JOSH AND ABBY, THIS IS LUNA. TODAY IS HER FIRST DAY AS A BUG SCOUT.
YAY!

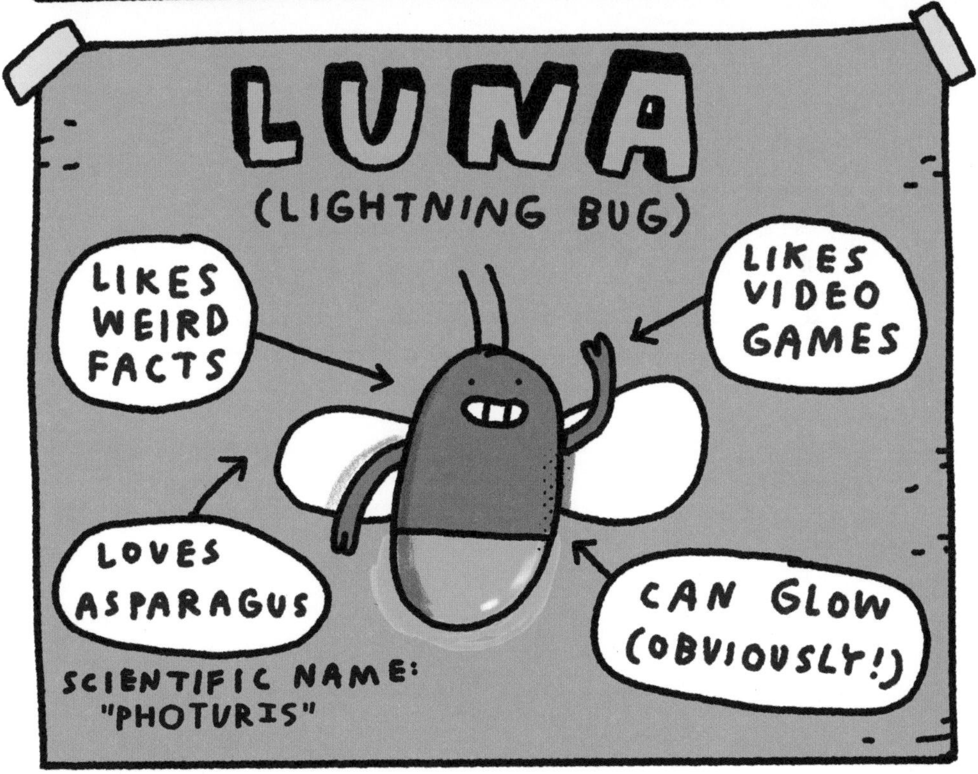
LUNA
(LIGHTNING BUG)
LIKES WEIRD FACTS
LIKES VIDEO GAMES
LOVES ASPARAGUS
CAN GLOW (OBVIOUSLY!)
SCIENTIFIC NAME: "PHOTURIS"

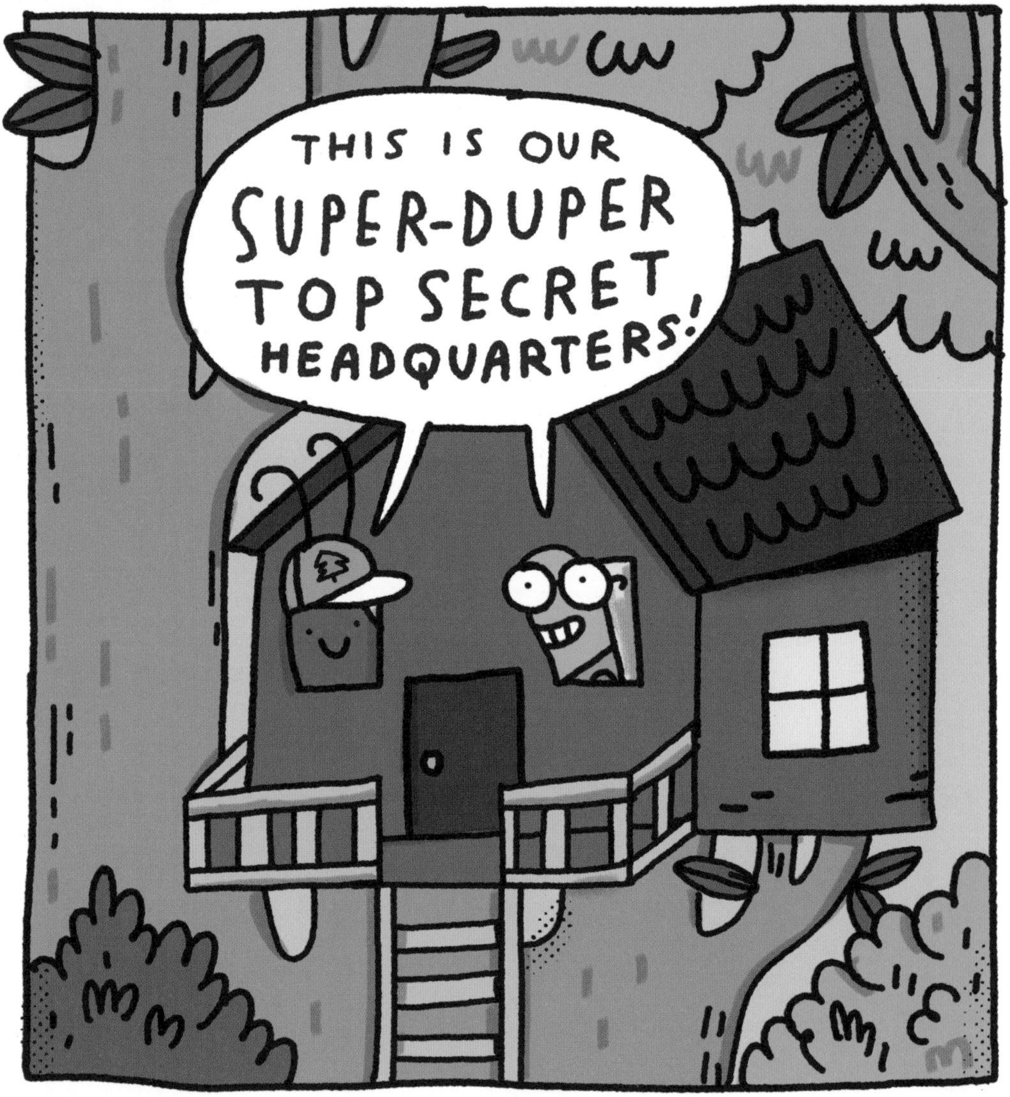
THIS IS OUR SUPER-DUPER TOP SECRET HEADQUARTERS!

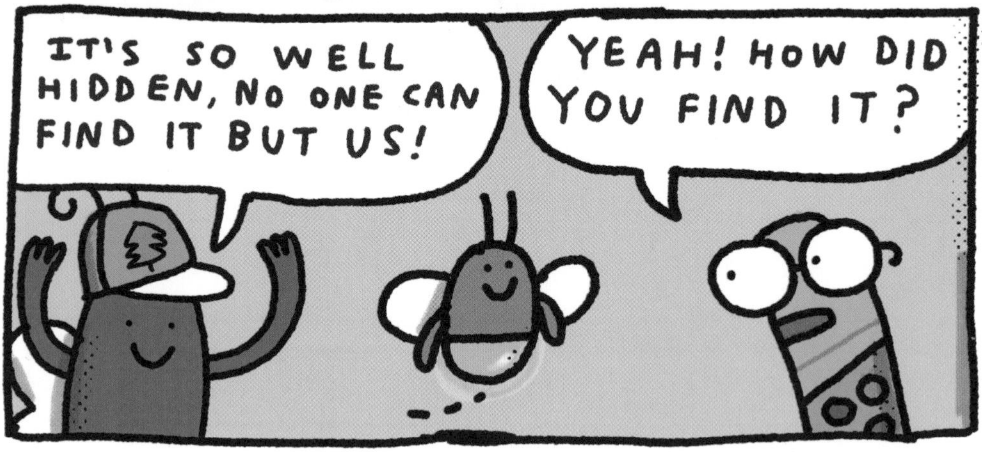
IT'S SO WELL HIDDEN, NO ONE CAN FIND IT BUT US!
YEAH! HOW DID YOU FIND IT?

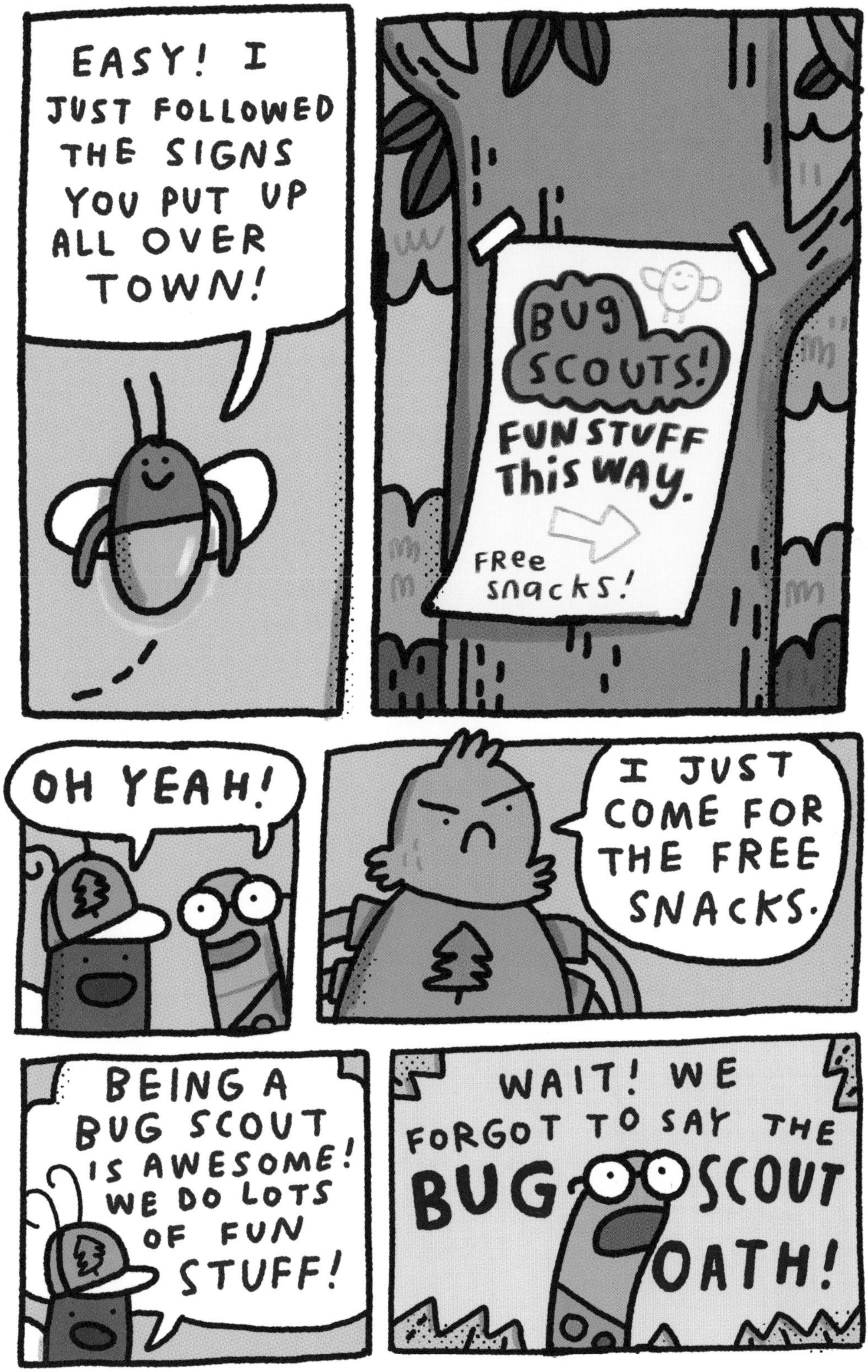
EASY! I JUST FOLLOWED THE SIGNS YOU PUT UP ALL OVER TOWN!
BUG SCOUTS!
FUN STUFF This WAY.
FREE snacks!
OH YEAH!
I JUST COME FOR THE FREE SNACKS.
BEING A BUG SCOUT IS AWESOME! WE DO LOTS OF FUN STUFF!
WAIT! WE FORGOT TO SAY THE BUG SCOUT OATH!

THE OFFICIAL
BUG SCOUT
⊱⊱⊱ OATH ⊰⊰⊰

(READ THIS LOUDLY IN
YOUR BEST BUG VOICE!)

ALL BUGS ARE AWESOME
AND THAT IS A FACT.

RAISE YOUR LEG OR ANTENNA
AND LET'S MAKE A PACT.

I PROMISE TO FLY, I PROMISE
TO CRAWL, OR MAKE A COOL
WEB, OR ROLL INTO A BALL.

I VOW TO ALWAYS BE DIGGING
IN DIRT AND SOMETIMES GROW
NEW PARTS WHEN I'M HURT.

I CAN BE SLIMY AND
SOMETIMES I STING.
MAYBE I SCURRY OR
FLY WITH MY WINGS.

I PLEDGE TO BE BRAVE
AND ADVENTUROUS, TOO.

AND DO ALL OF THE THINGS
THAT BUGS LIKE TO DO!

CHAPTER 2

BUG BADGES!

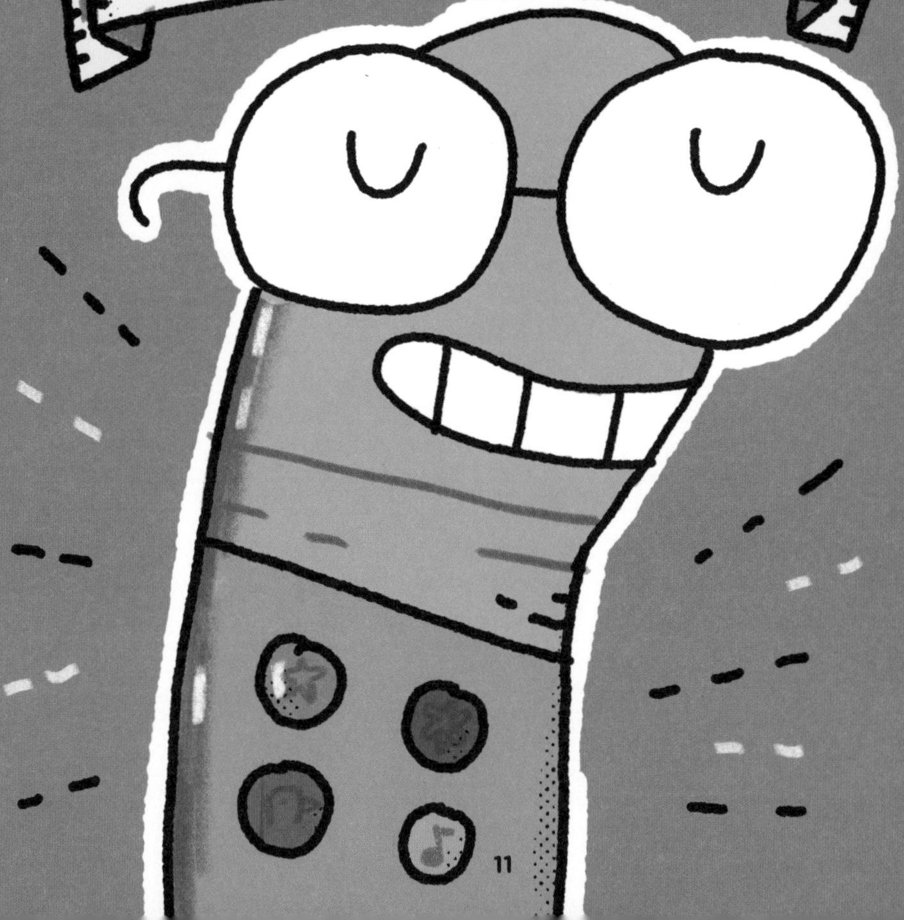

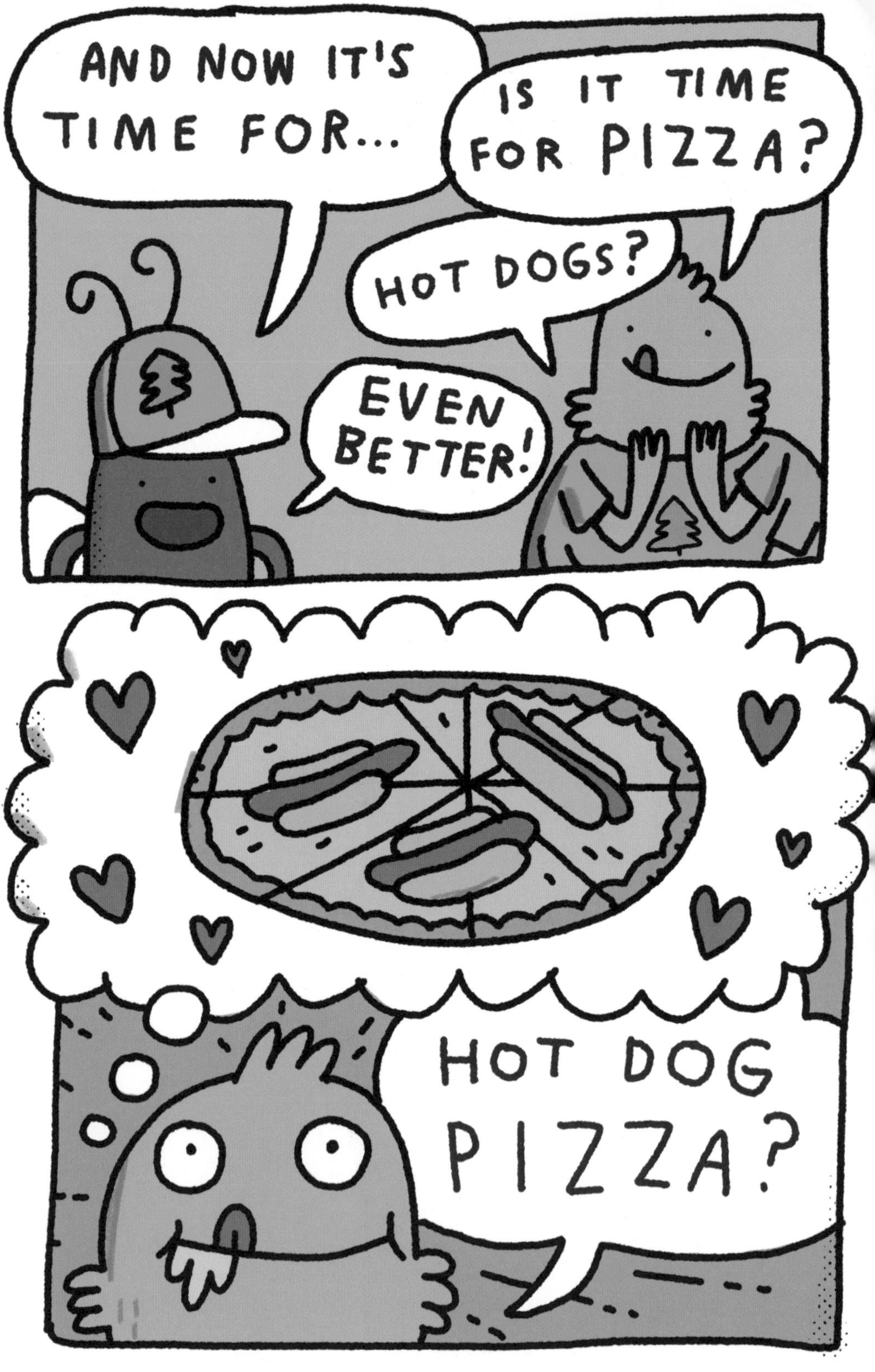
AND NOW IT'S TIME FOR...
IS IT TIME FOR PIZZA?
HOT DOGS?
EVEN BETTER!
HOT DOG PIZZA?

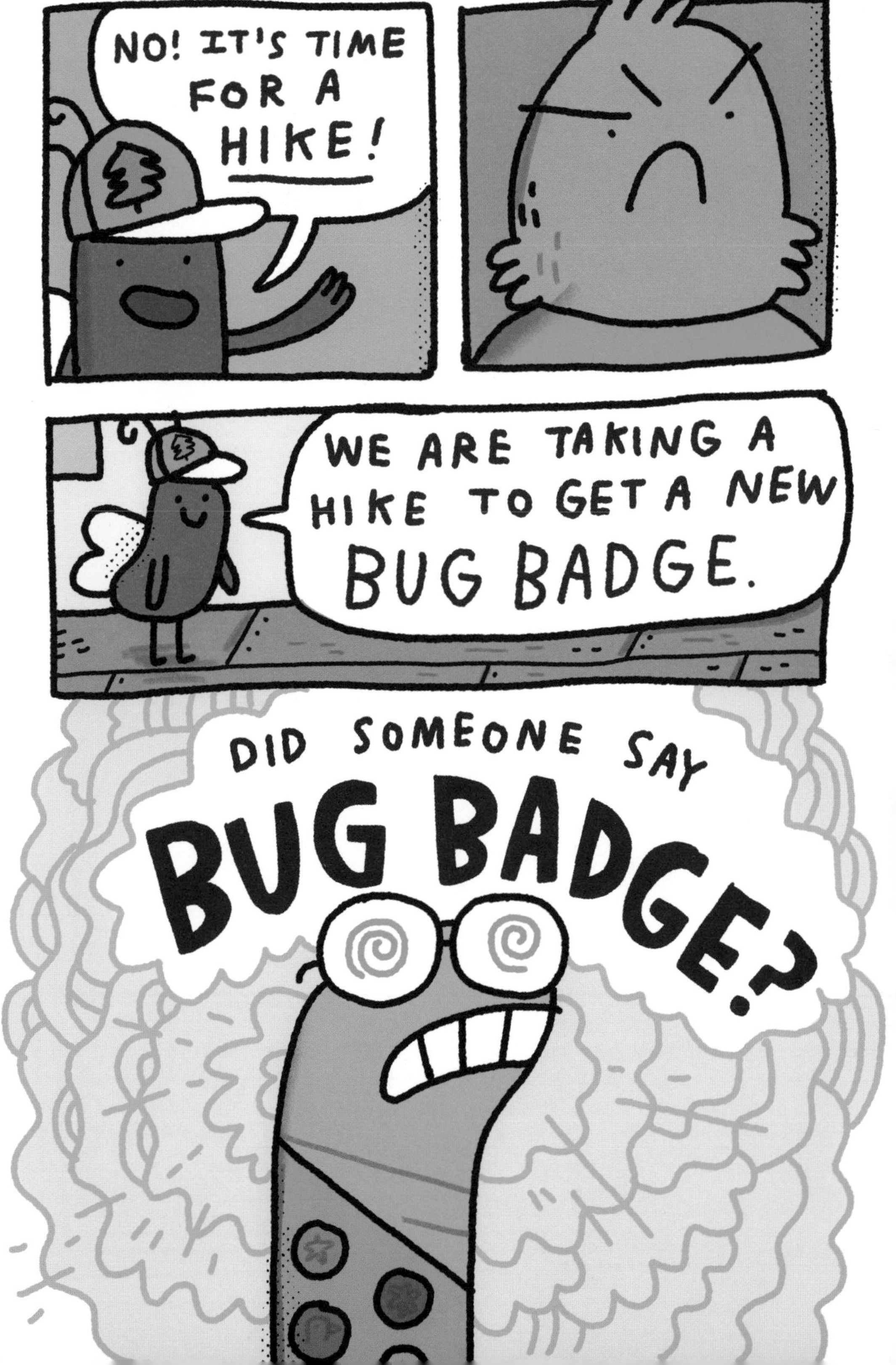
NO! IT'S TIME FOR A HIKE!
WE ARE TAKING A HIKE TO GET A NEW BUG BADGE.
DID SOMEONE SAY BUG BADGE?

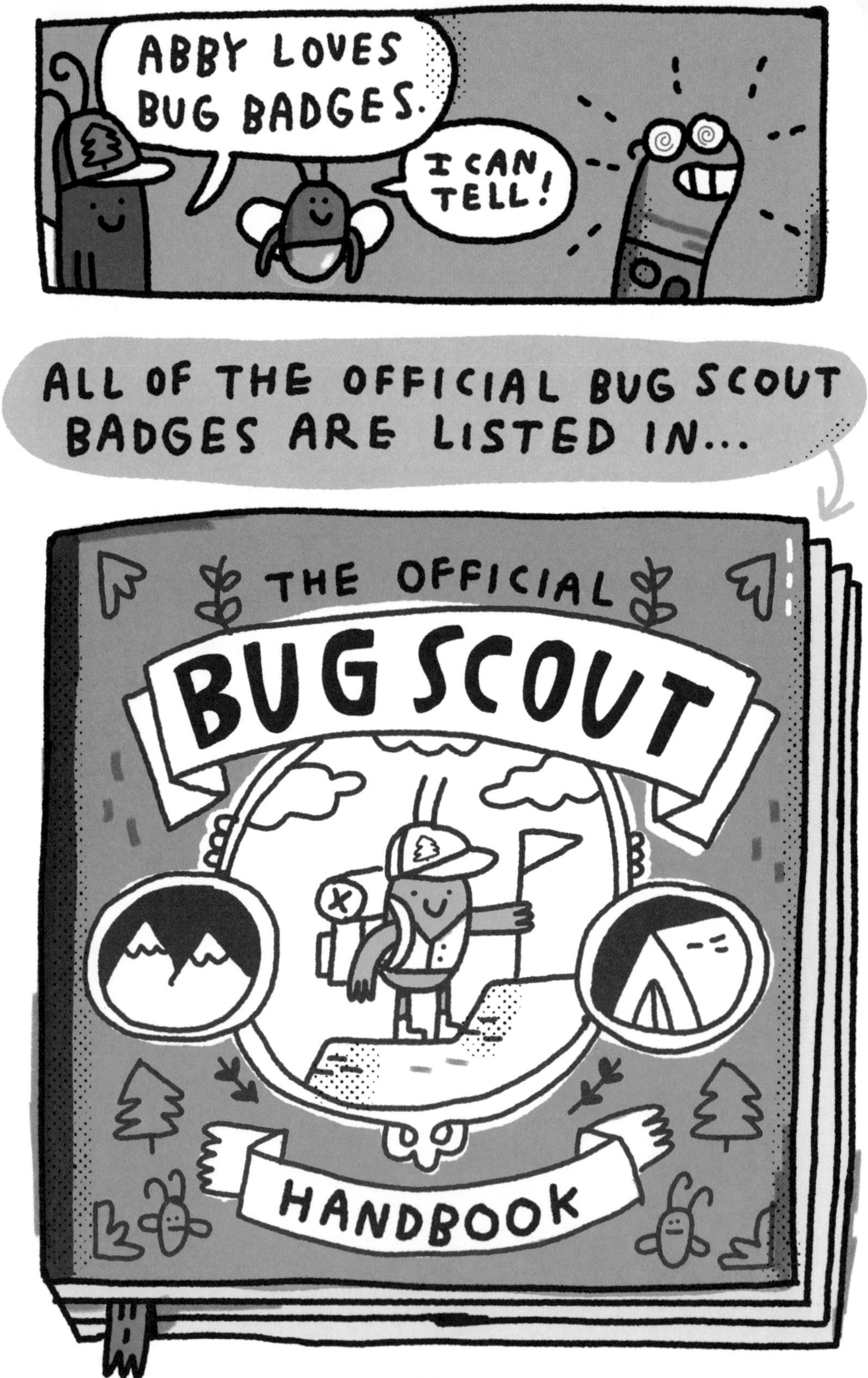
ABBY LOVES BUG BADGES.
I CAN TELL!
ALL OF THE OFFICIAL BUG SCOUT BADGES ARE LISTED IN...
THE OFFICIAL BUG SCOUT HANDBOOK

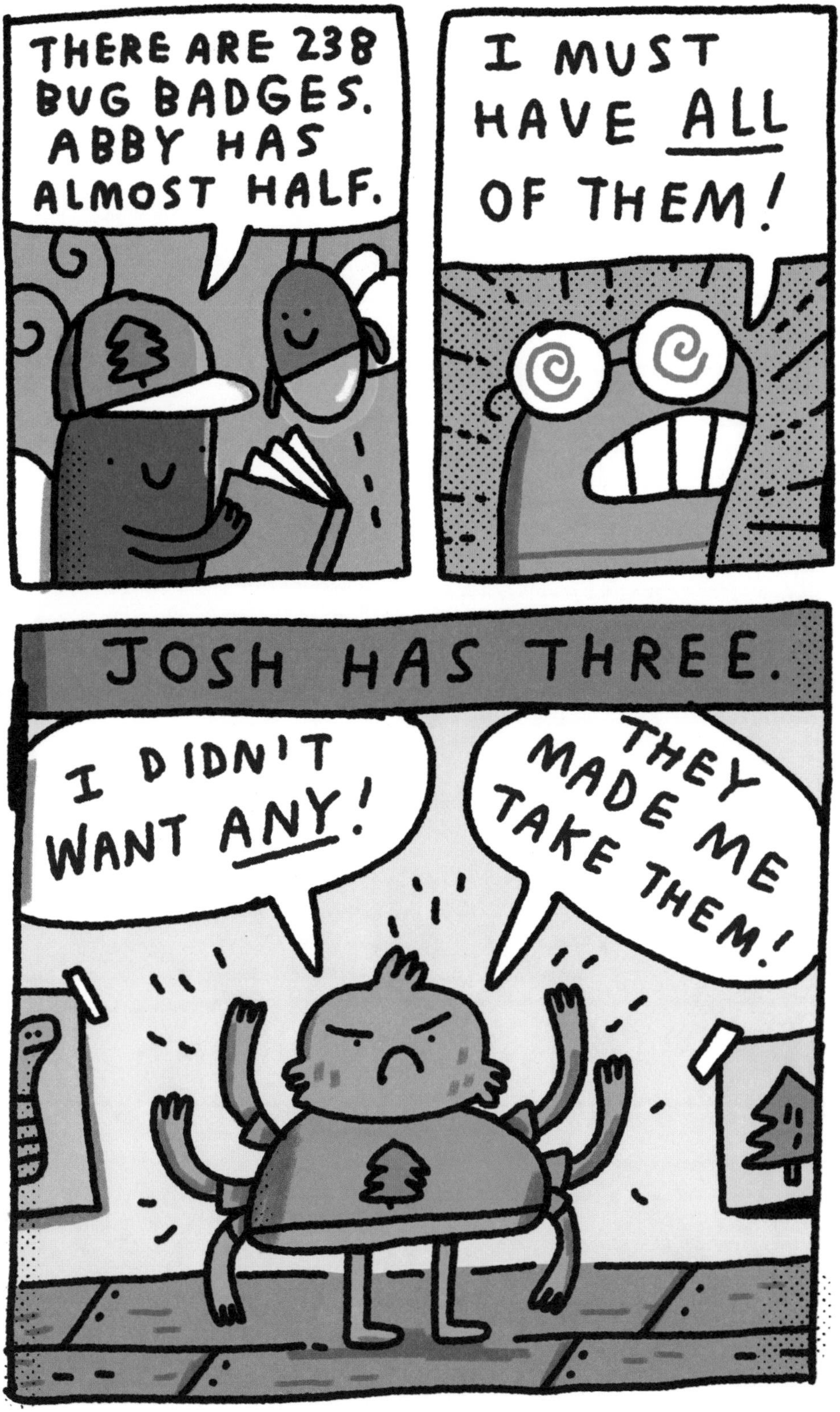
THERE ARE 238 BUG BADGES. ABBY HAS ALMOST HALF.
I MUST HAVE ALL OF THEM!
JOSH HAS THREE.
I DIDN'T WANT ANY!
THEY MADE ME TAKE THEM!

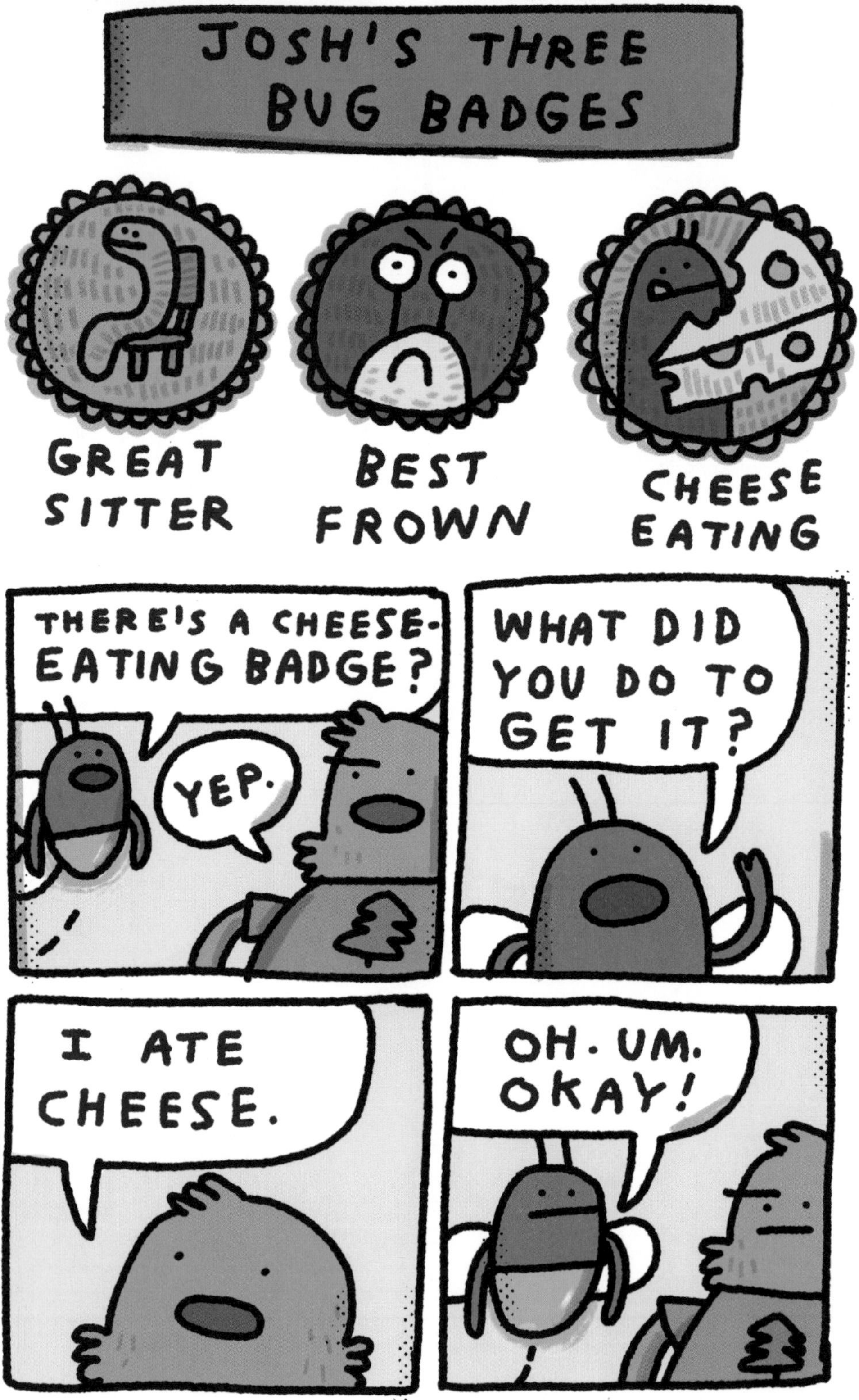
JOSH'S THREE BUG BADGES
GREAT SITTER
BEST FROWN
CHEESE EATING
THERE'S A CHEESE-EATING BADGE?
YEP.
WHAT DID YOU DO TO GET IT?
I ATE CHEESE.
OH. UM. OKAY!

A FEW OF ABBY'S FAVORITE BUG BADGES

TREE HUGGING

SWIMMING

SCIENCE

FRIENDSHIP

UFO WATCHING

KNITTING

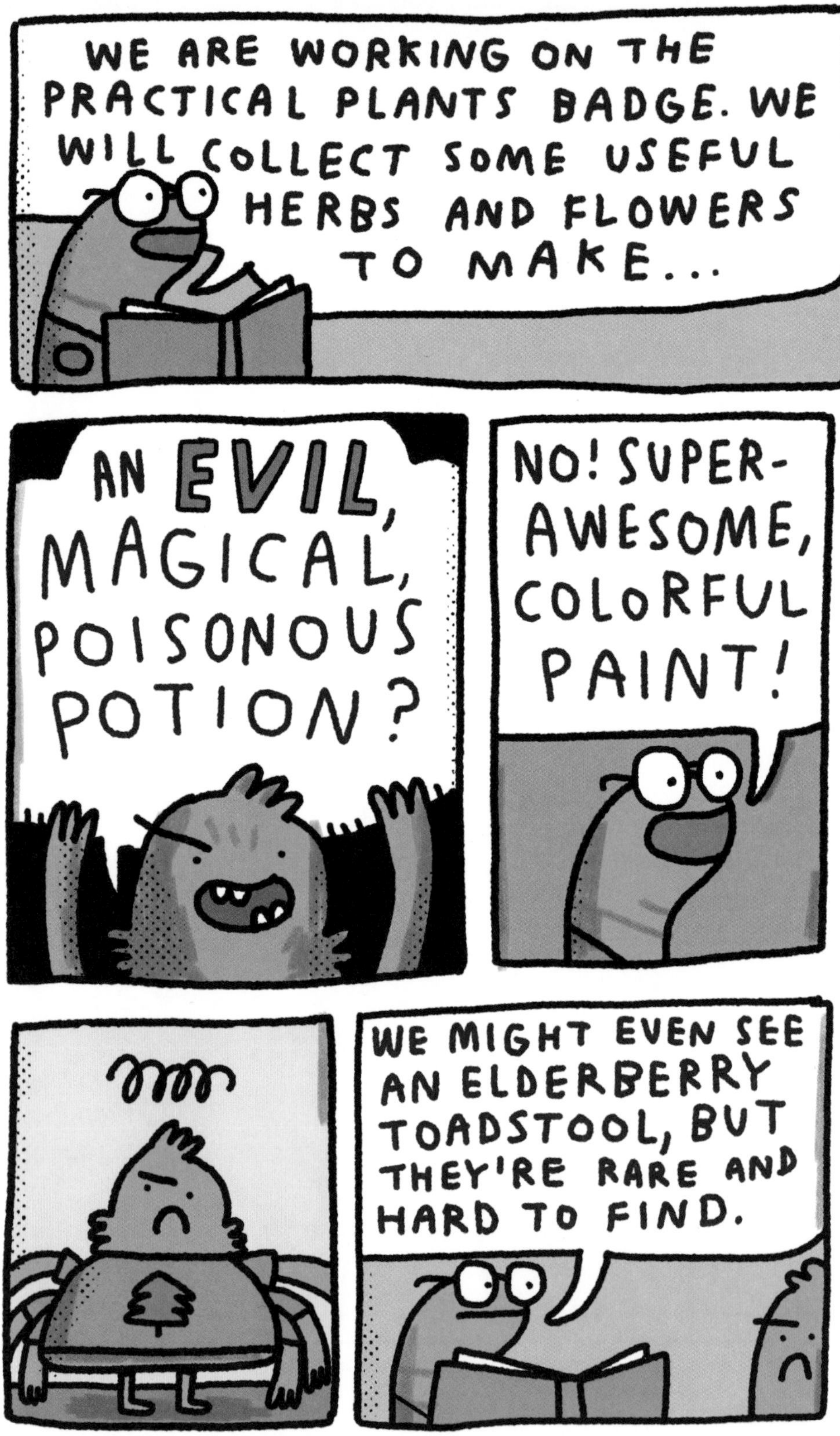
WE ARE WORKING ON THE PRACTICAL PLANTS BADGE. WE WILL COLLECT SOME USEFUL HERBS AND FLOWERS TO MAKE...
AN EVIL, MAGICAL, POISONOUS POTION?
NO! SUPER-AWESOME, COLORFUL PAINT!
WE MIGHT EVEN SEE AN ELDERBERRY TOADSTOOL, BUT THEY'RE RARE AND HARD TO FIND.

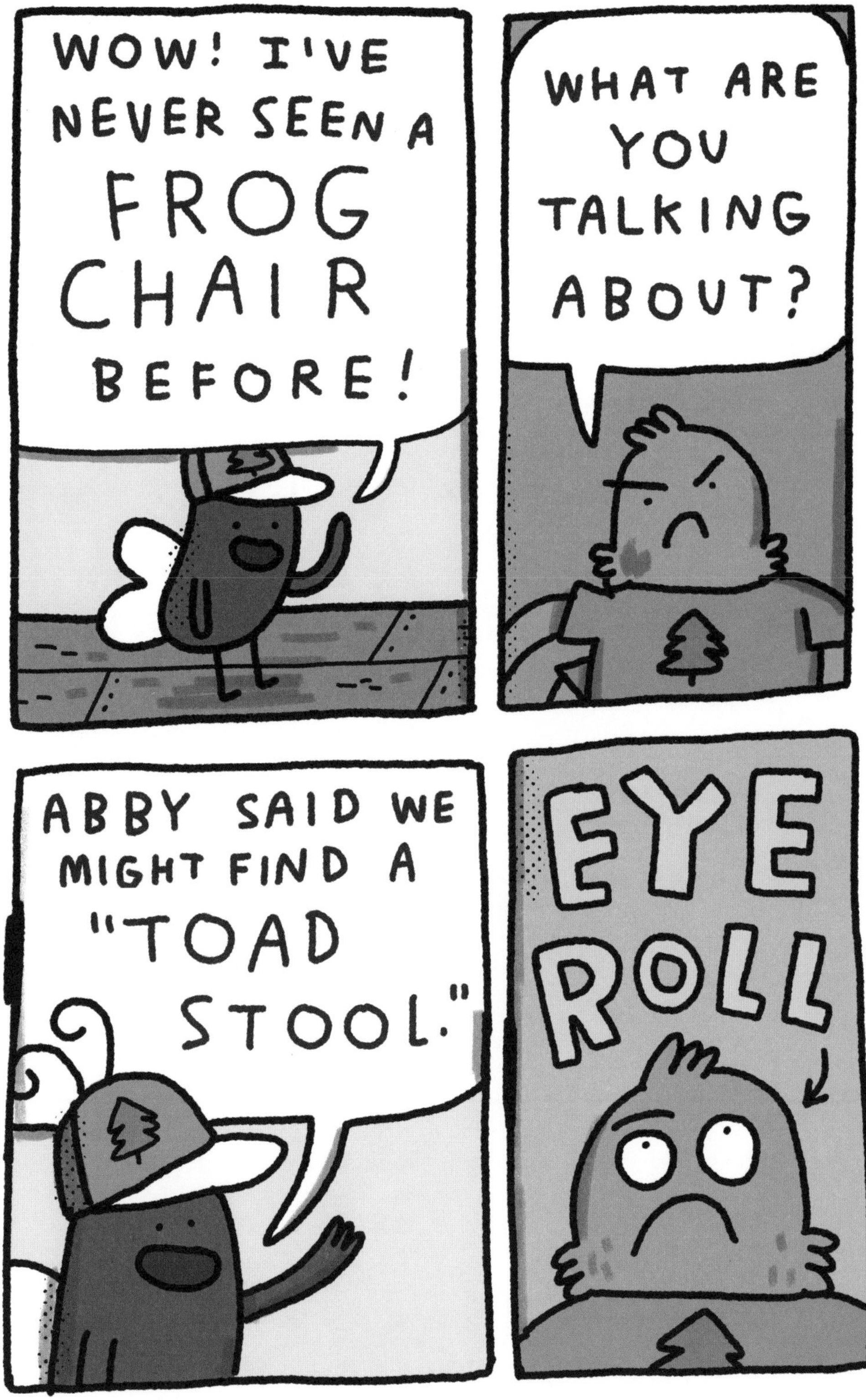
WOW! I'VE NEVER SEEN A FROG CHAIR BEFORE!
WHAT ARE YOU TALKING ABOUT?
ABBY SAID WE MIGHT FIND A "TOAD STOOL."
EYE ROLL

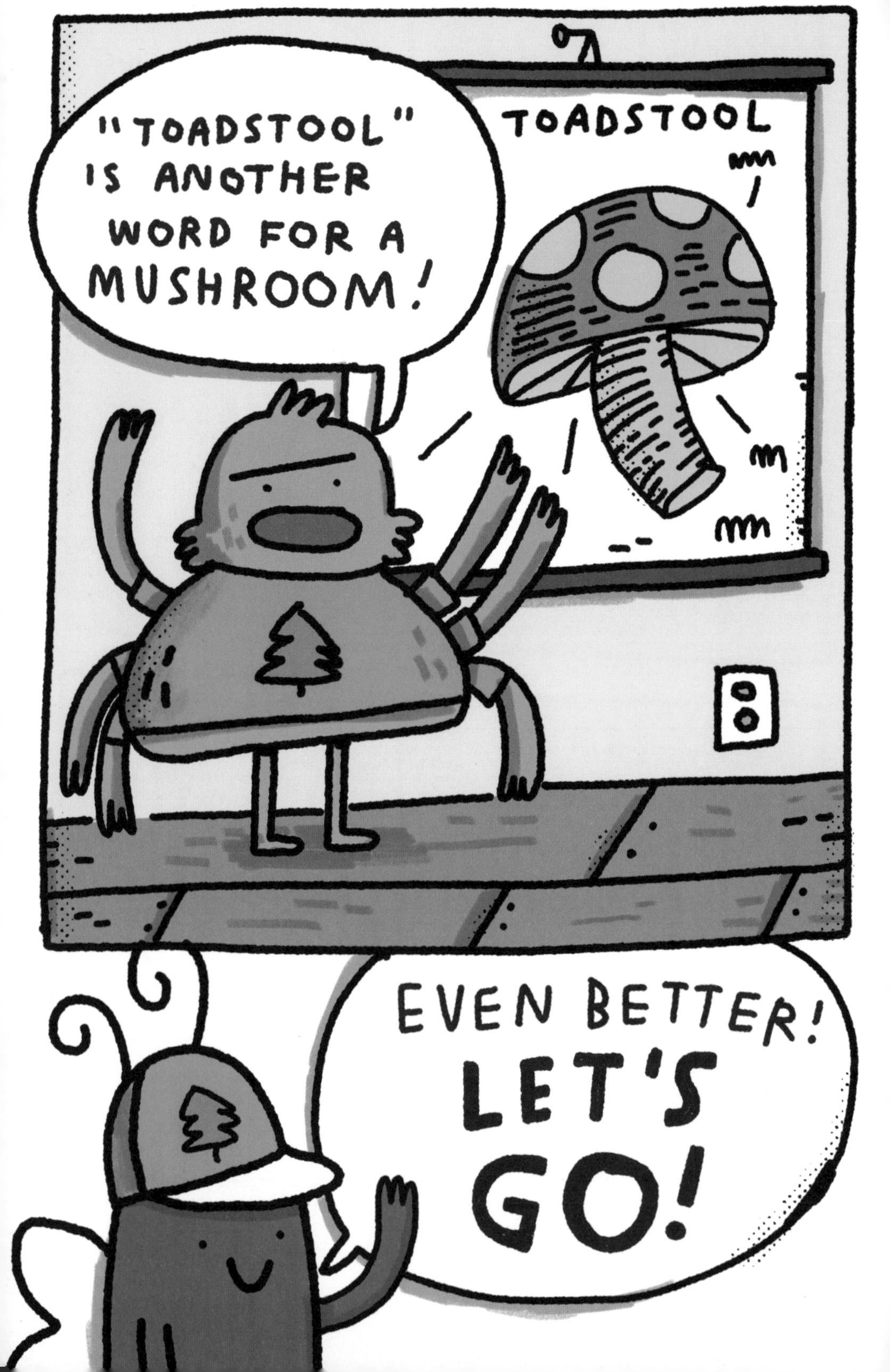
"TOADSTOOL" IS ANOTHER WORD FOR A MUSHROOM!
TOADSTOOL
EVEN BETTER! LET'S GO!

CHAPTER 3

FORAGING

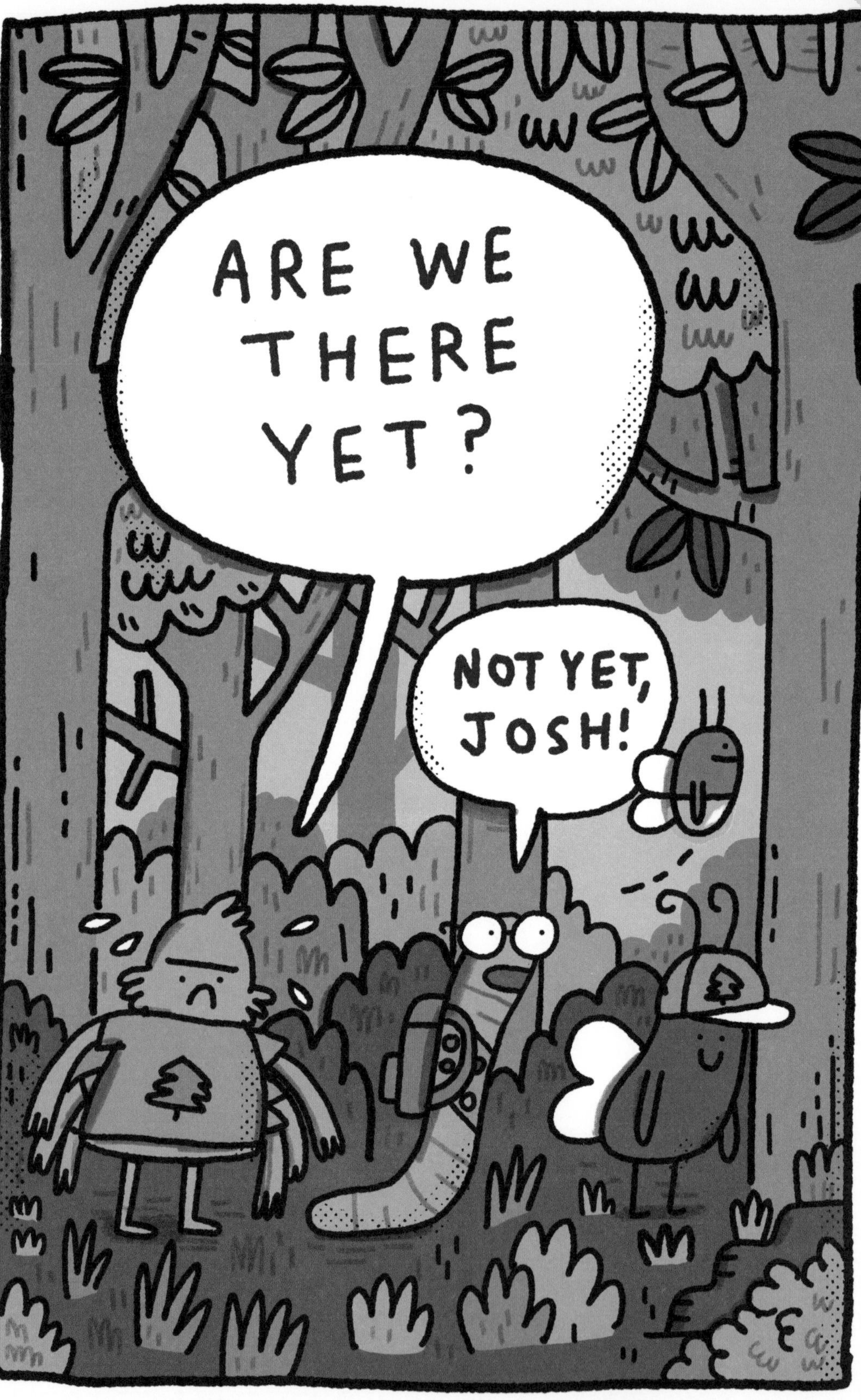
ARE WE THERE YET?
NOT YET, JOSH!

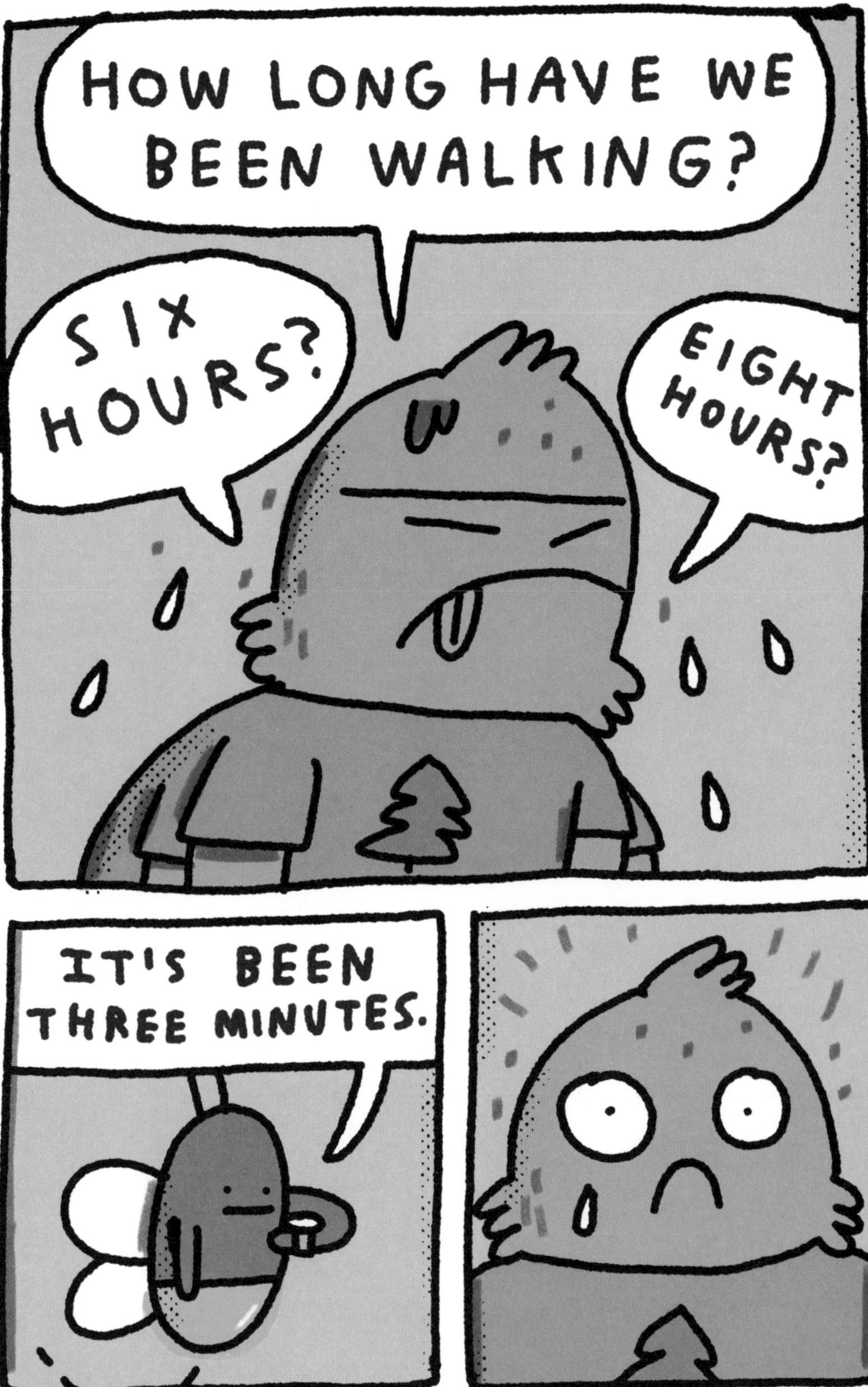
HOW LONG HAVE WE BEEN WALKING?
SIX HOURS?
EIGHT HOURS?
IT'S BEEN THREE MINUTES.

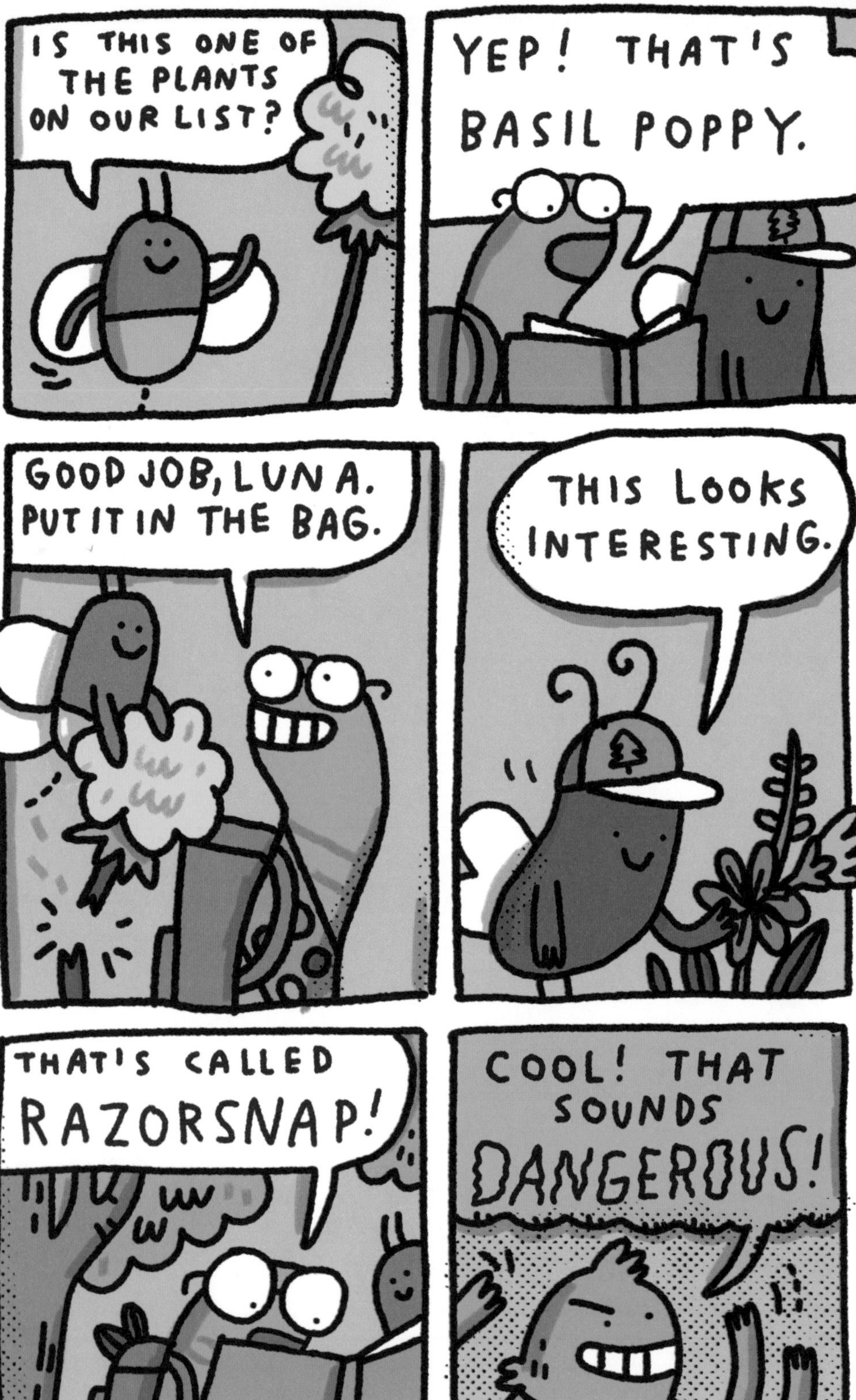
IS THIS ONE OF THE PLANTS ON OUR LIST?
YEP! THAT'S BASIL POPPY.
GOOD JOB, LUNA. PUT IT IN THE BAG.
THIS LOOKS INTERESTING.
THAT'S CALLED RAZORSNAP!
COOL! THAT SOUNDS DANGEROUS!

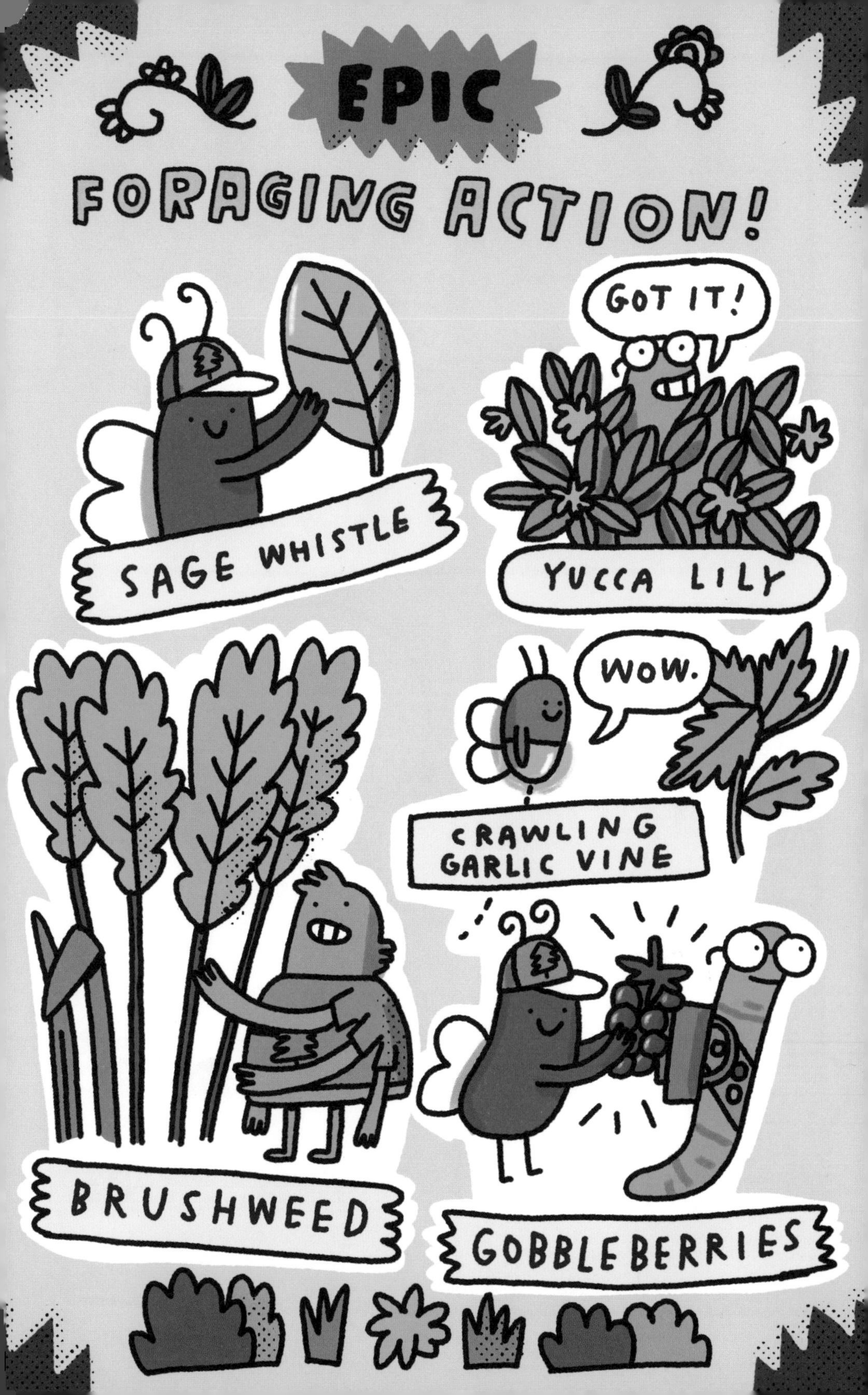
EPIC
FORAGING ACTION!
SAGE WHISTLE
GOT IT!
YUCCA LILY
WOW.
CRAWLING GARLIC VINE
BRUSHWEED
GOBBLEBERRIES

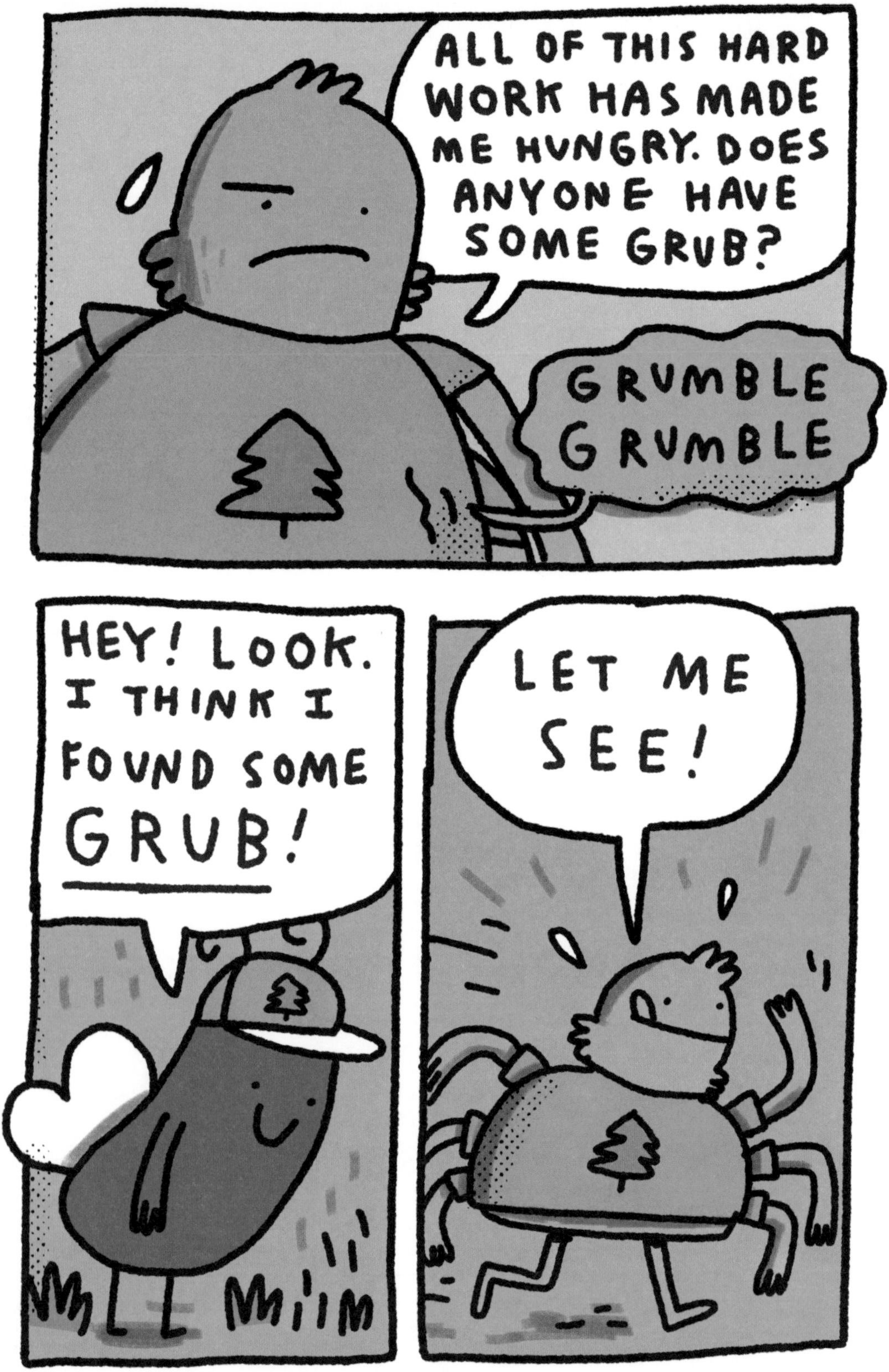
ALL OF THIS HARD WORK HAS MADE ME HUNGRY. DOES ANYONE HAVE SOME GRUB?
GRUMBLE GRUMBLE
HEY! LOOK. I THINK I FOUND SOME GRUB!
LET ME SEE!

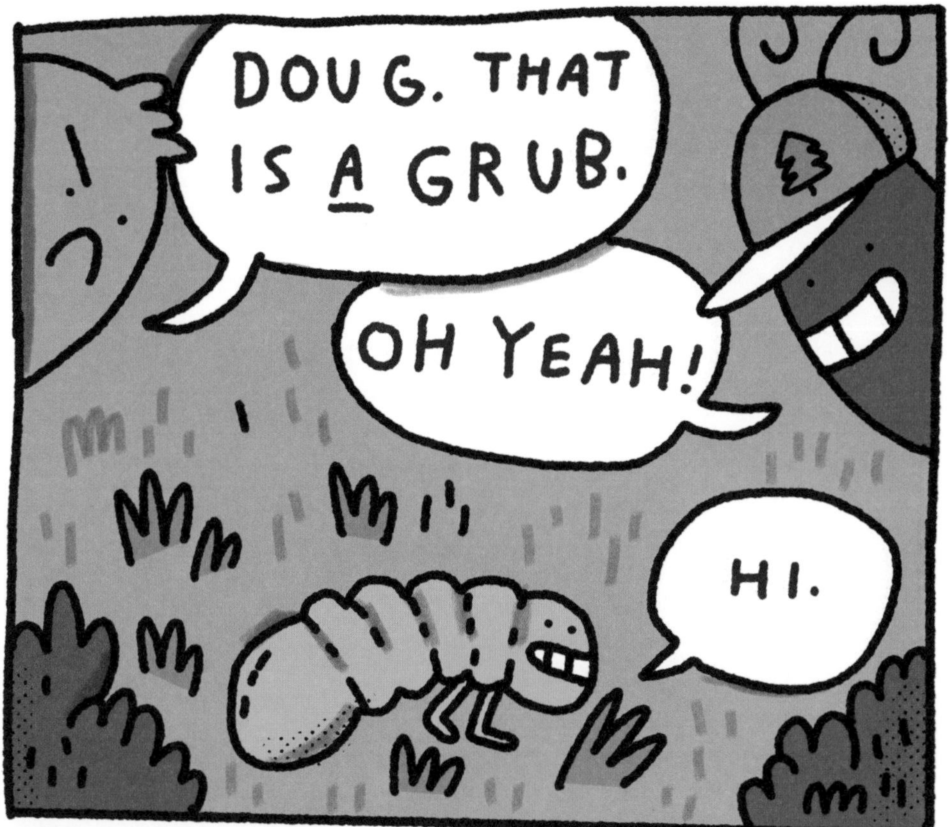
DOUG. THAT IS A GRUB.
OH YEAH!
HI.

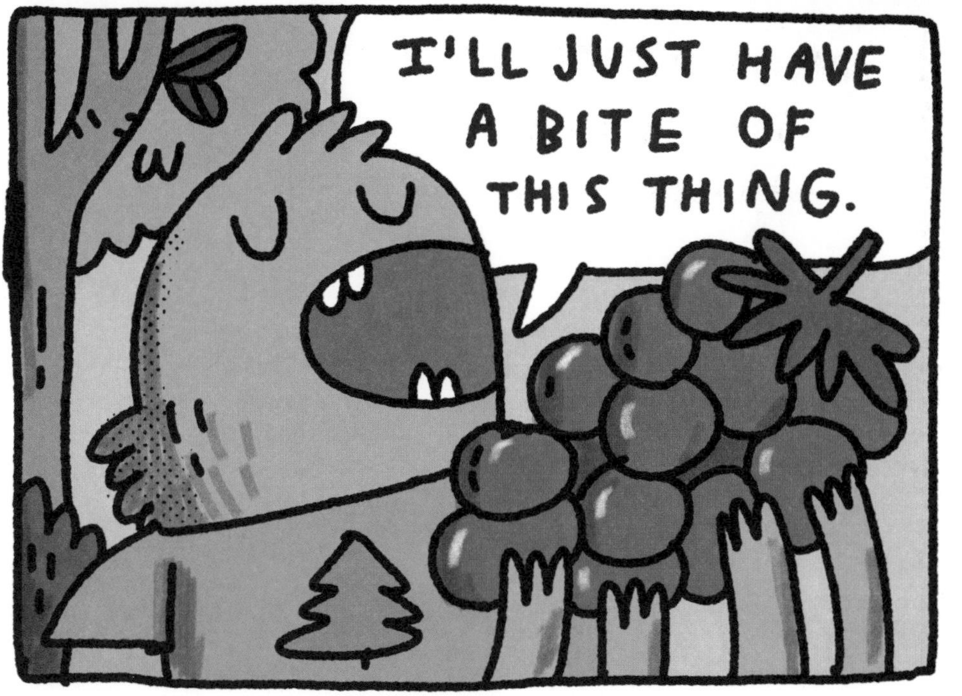
I'LL JUST HAVE A BITE OF THIS THING.

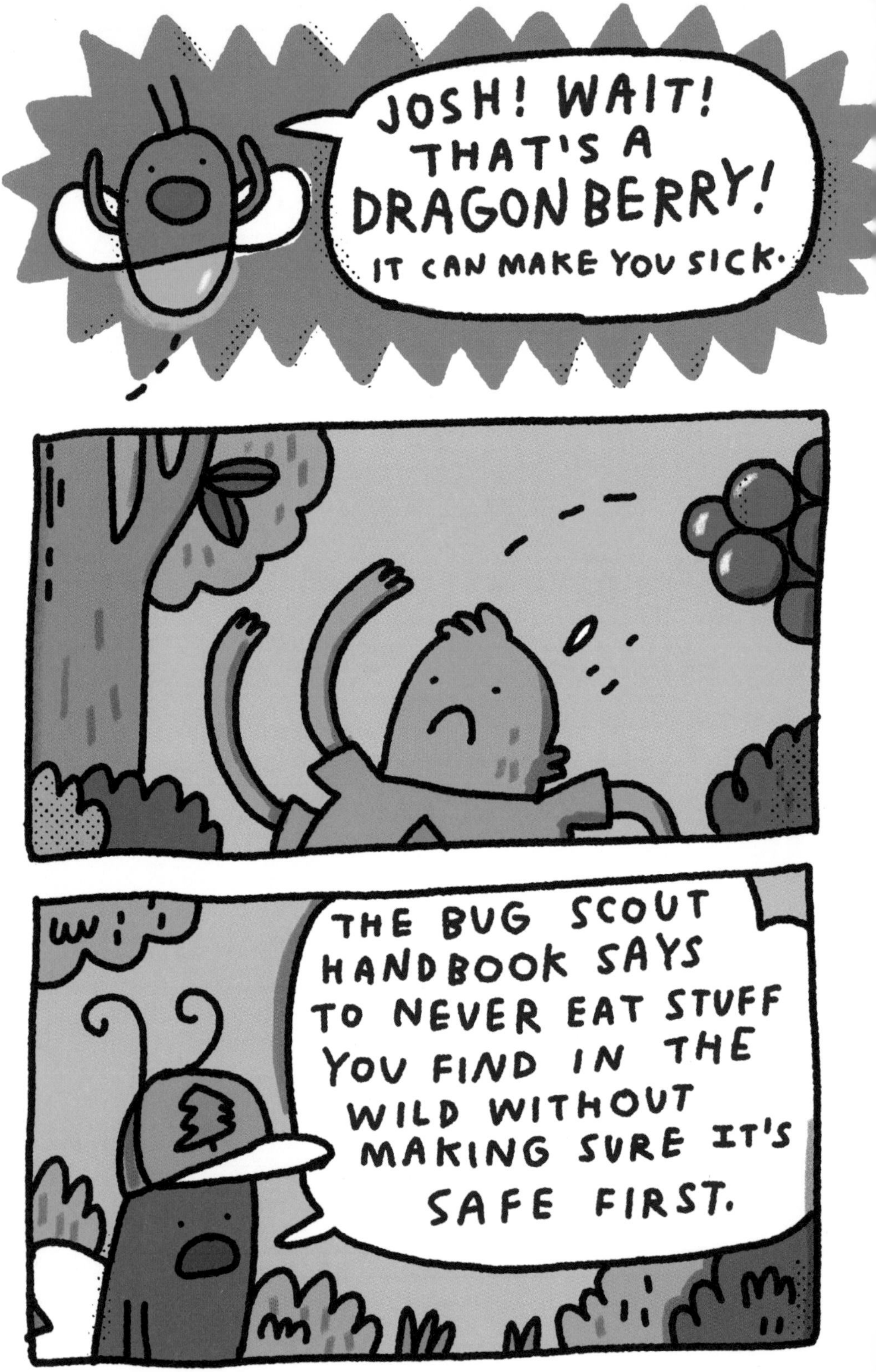
JOSH! WAIT! THAT'S A DRAGON BERRY! IT CAN MAKE YOU SICK.
THE BUG SCOUT HANDBOOK SAYS TO NEVER EAT STUFF YOU FIND IN THE WILD WITHOUT MAKING SURE IT'S SAFE FIRST.

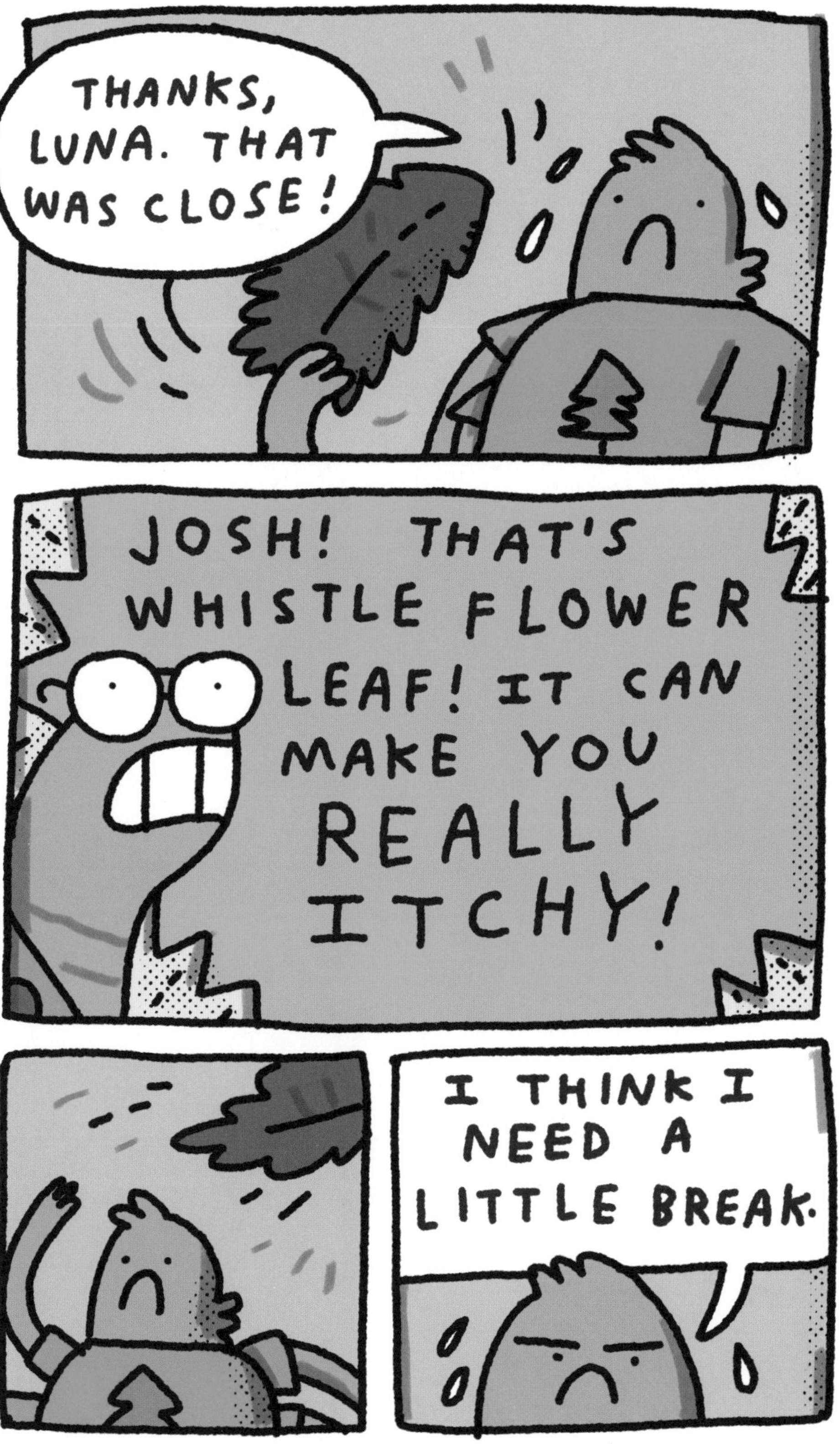
THANKS, LUNA. THAT WAS CLOSE!
JOSH! THAT'S WHISTLE FLOWER LEAF! IT CAN MAKE YOU REALLY ITCHY!
I THINK I NEED A LITTLE BREAK.

SPIDERWEB HAMMOCK TIME!

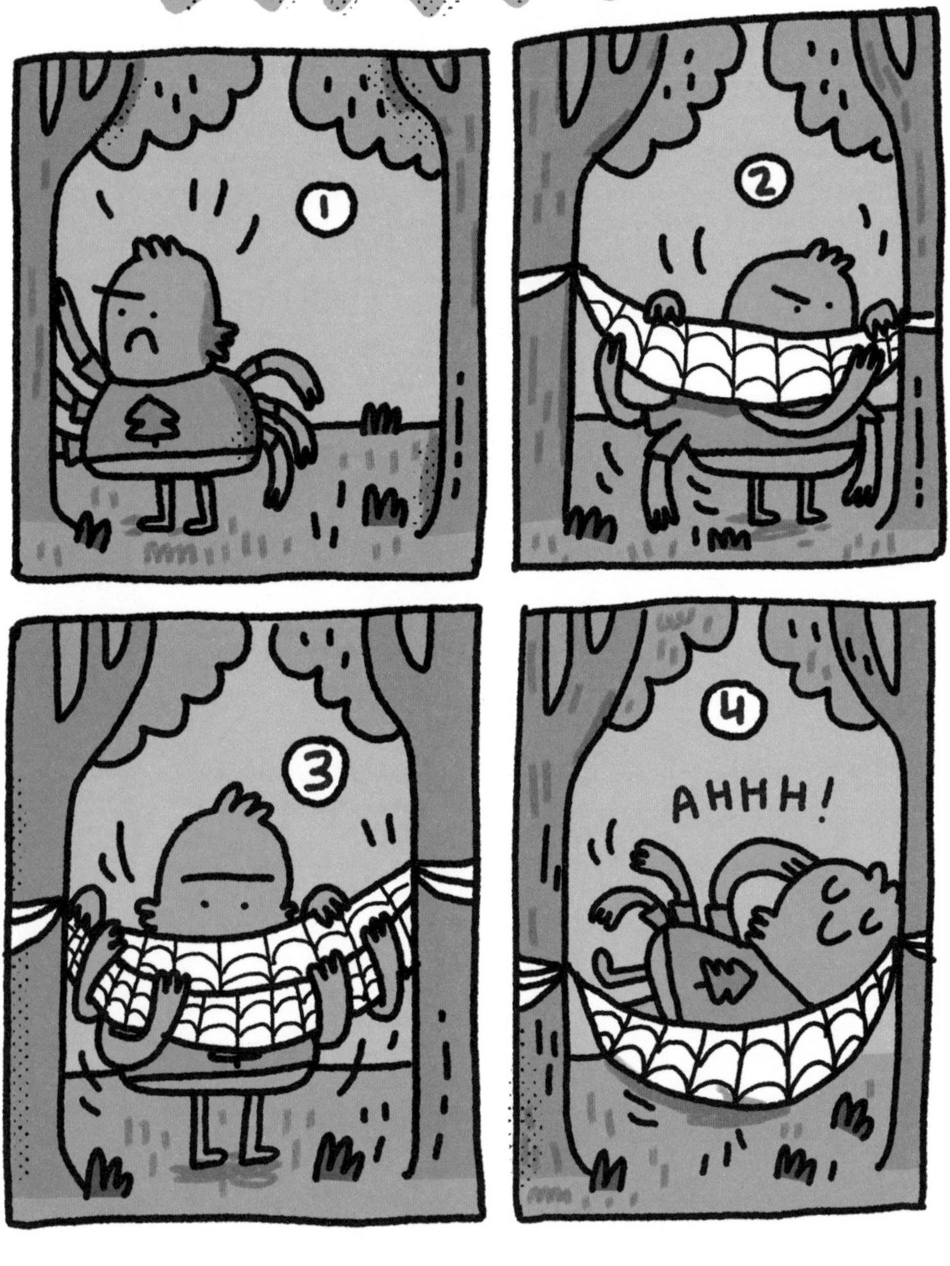
1
2
3
4
AHHH!

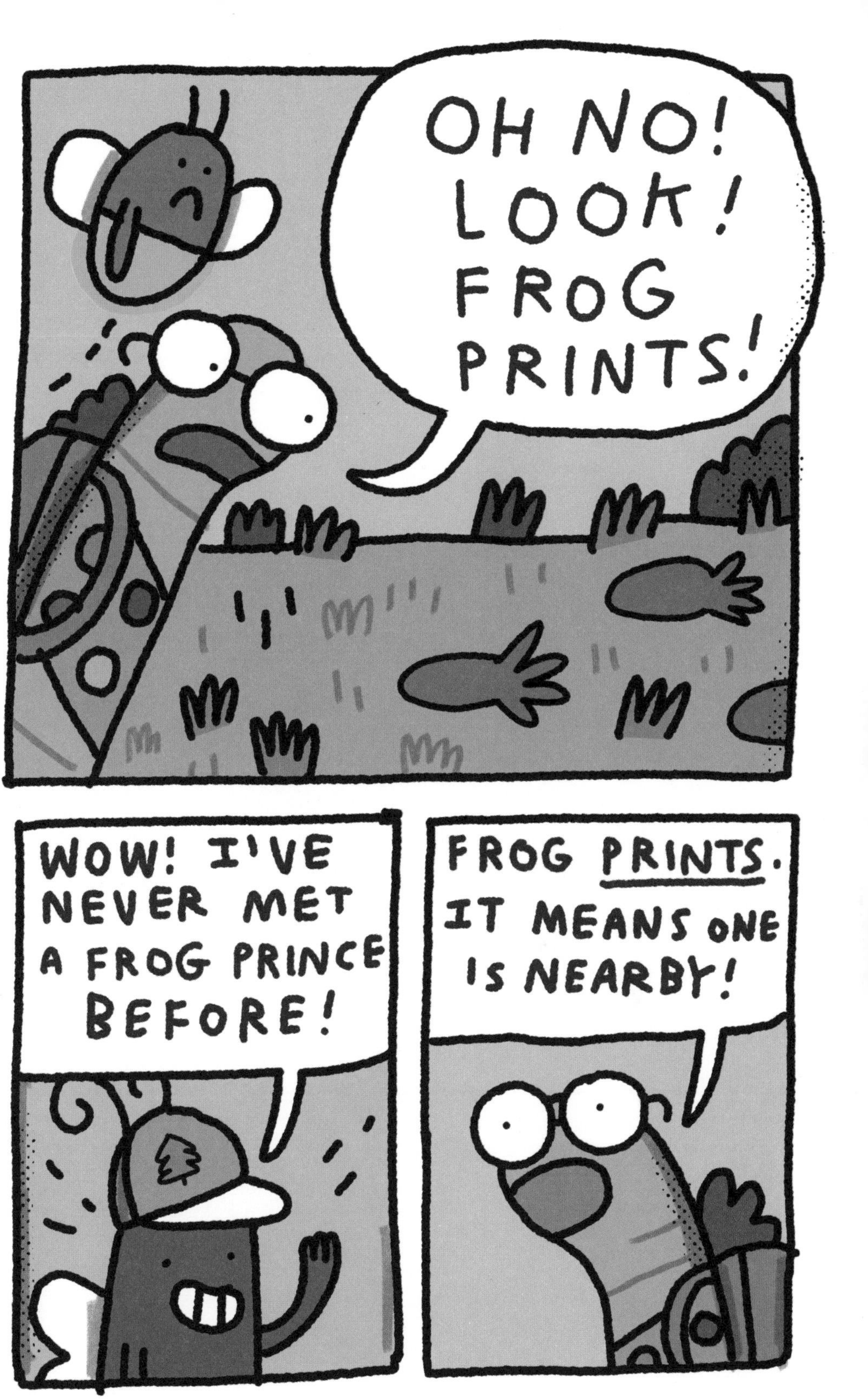
OH NO! LOOK! FROG PRINTS!
WOW! I'VE NEVER MET A FROG PRINCE BEFORE!
FROG PRINTS. IT MEANS ONE IS NEARBY!

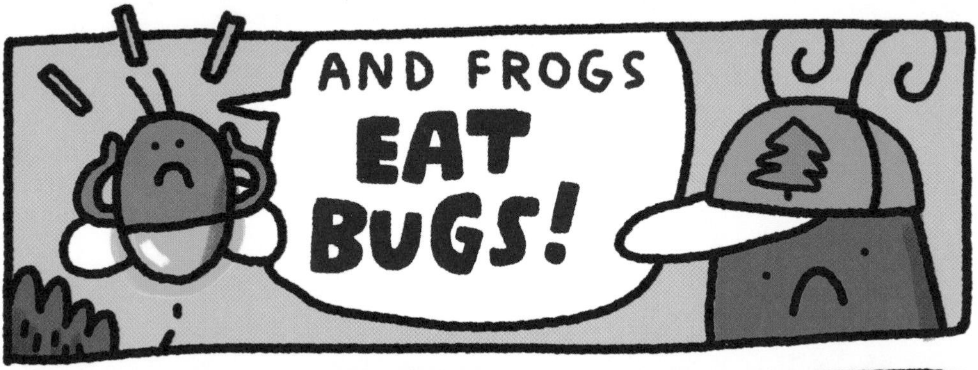
AND FROGS EAT BUGS!

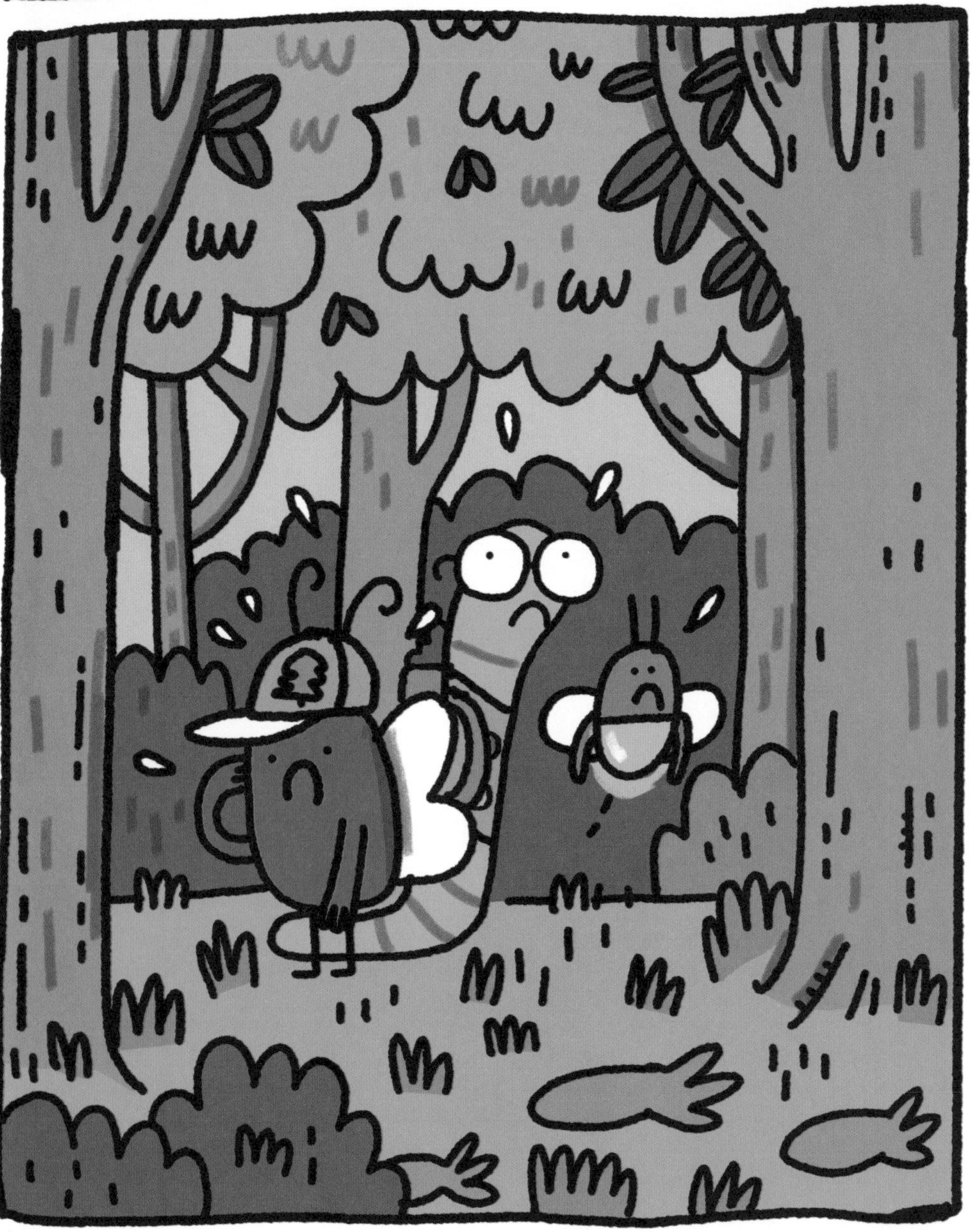

CHAPTER 4

RUN!

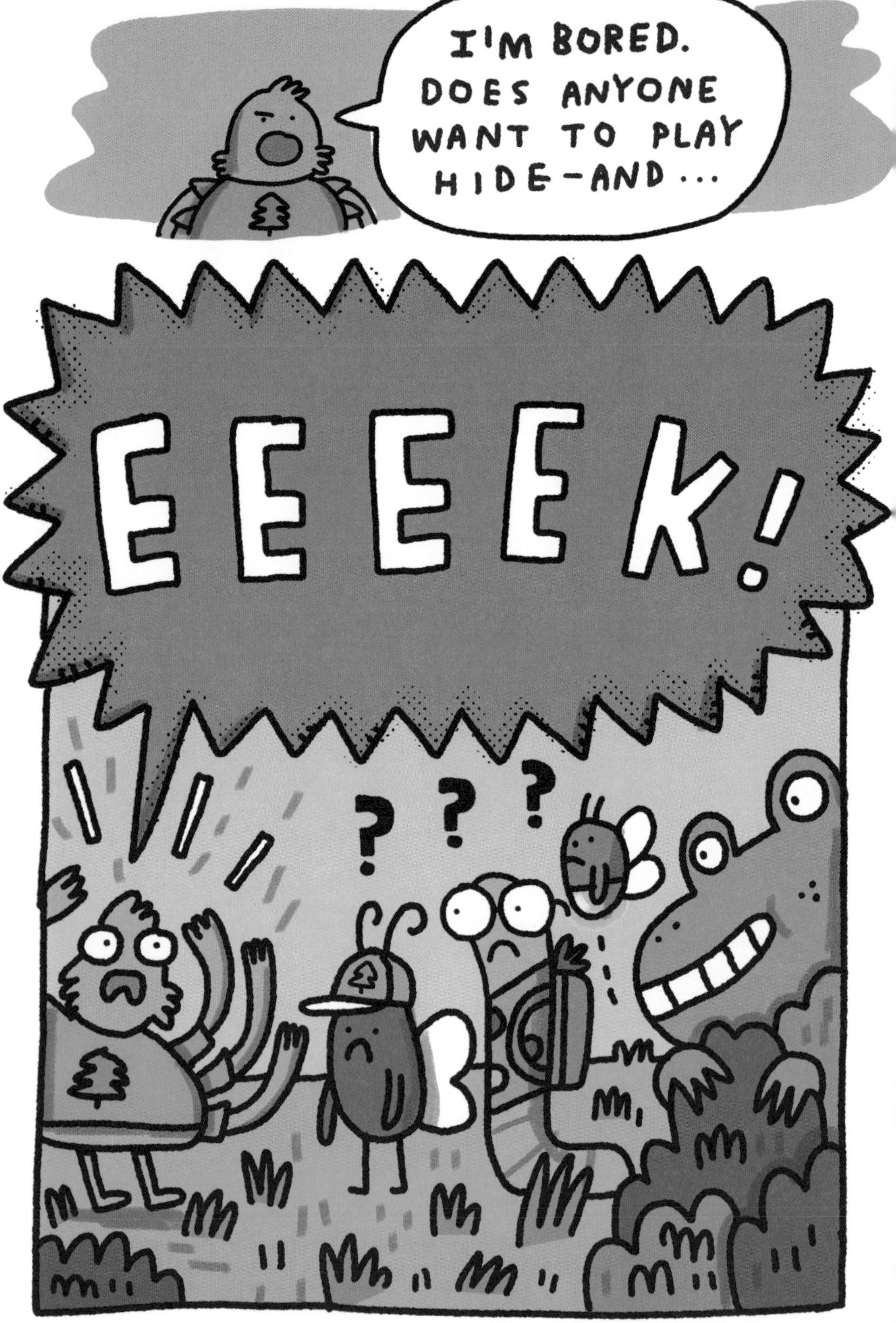
I'M BORED. DOES ANYONE WANT TO PLAY HIDE-AND...
EEEEK!
???

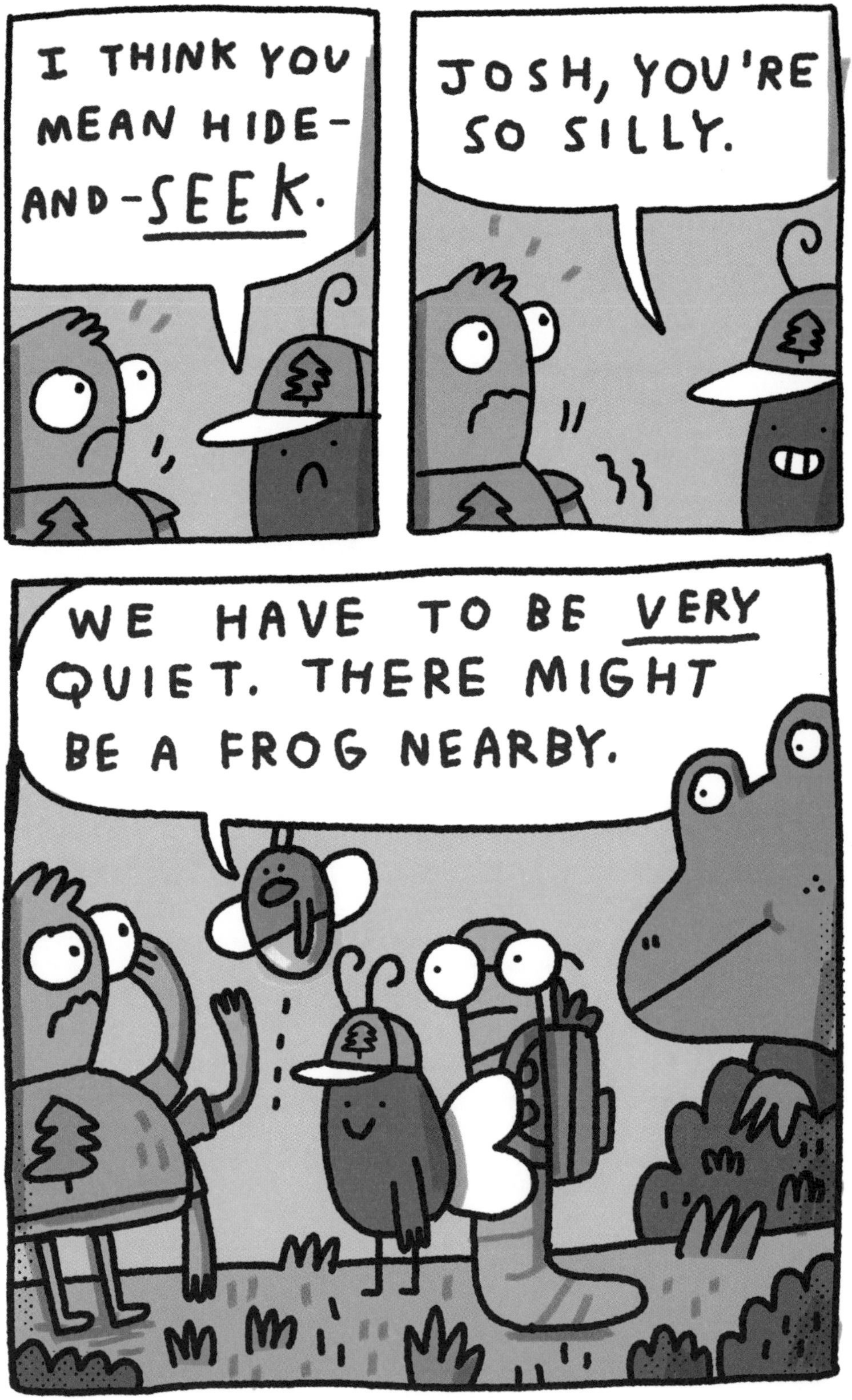
I THINK YOU MEAN HIDE-AND-SEEK.
JOSH, YOU'RE SO SILLY.
WE HAVE TO BE VERY QUIET. THERE MIGHT BE A FROG NEARBY.

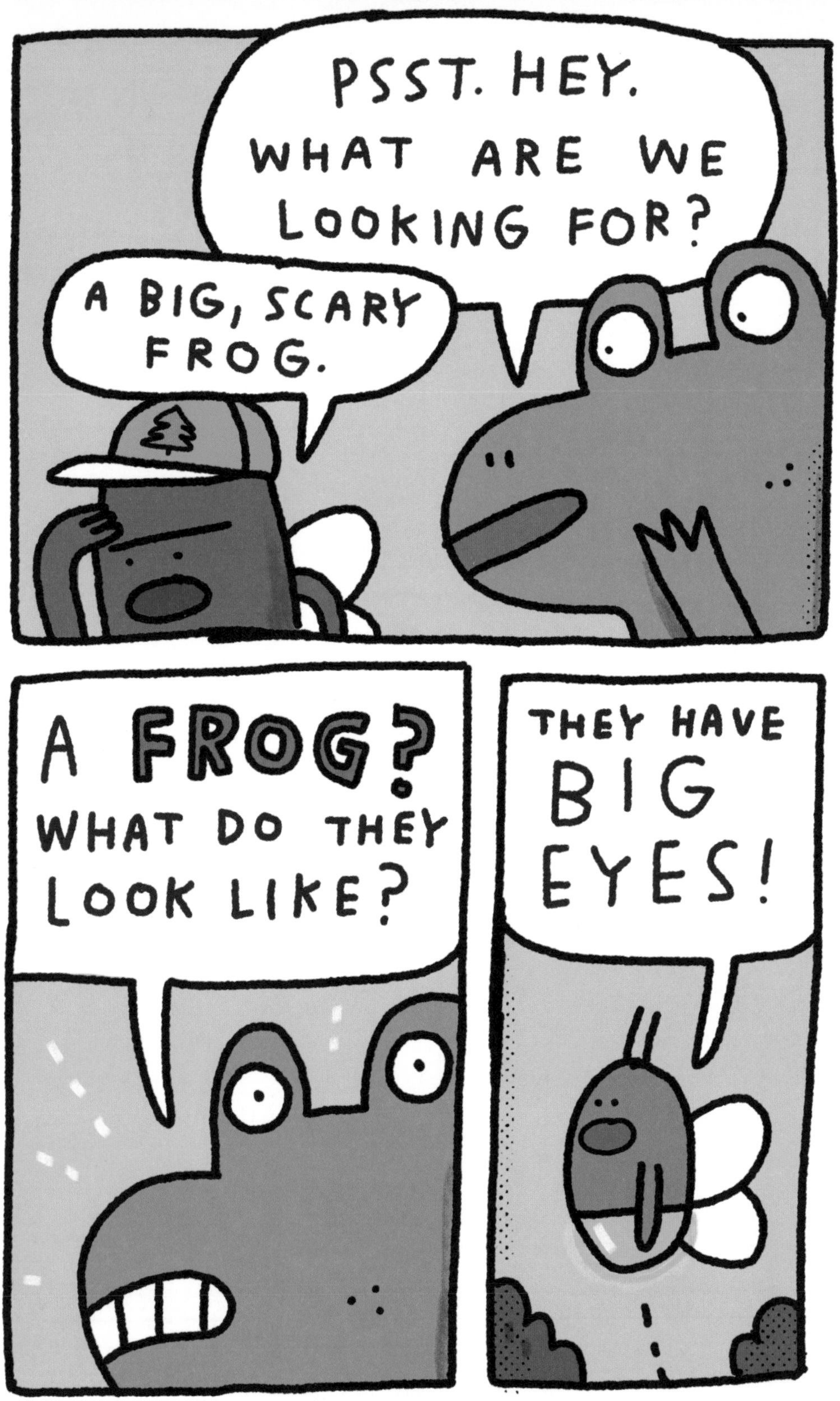
PSST. HEY. WHAT ARE WE LOOKING FOR?
A BIG, SCARY FROG.
A FROG? WHAT DO THEY LOOK LIKE?
THEY HAVE BIG EYES!

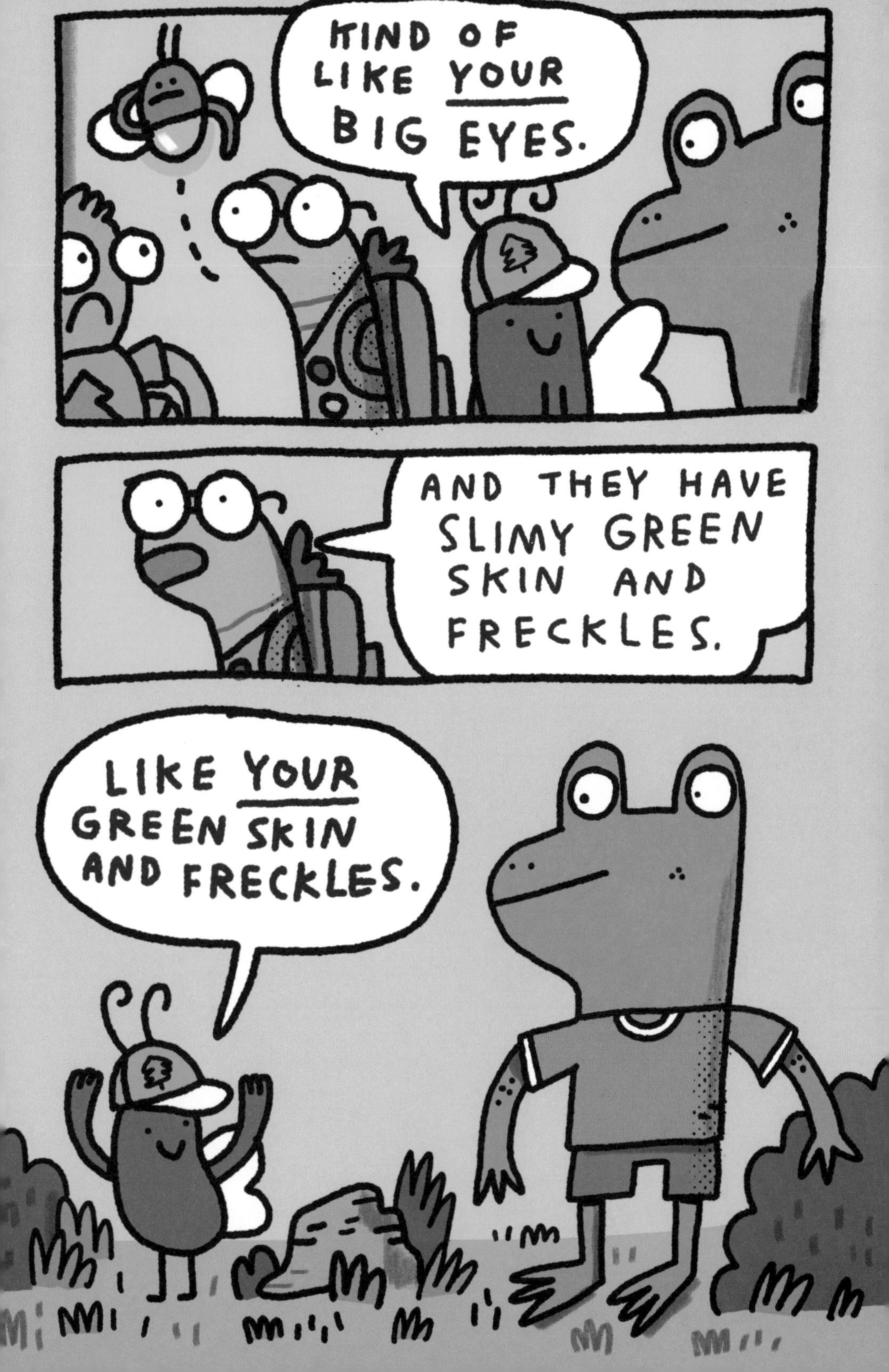
KIND OF LIKE YOUR BIG EYES.
AND THEY HAVE SLIMY GREEN SKIN AND FRECKLES.
LIKE YOUR GREEN SKIN AND FRECKLES.

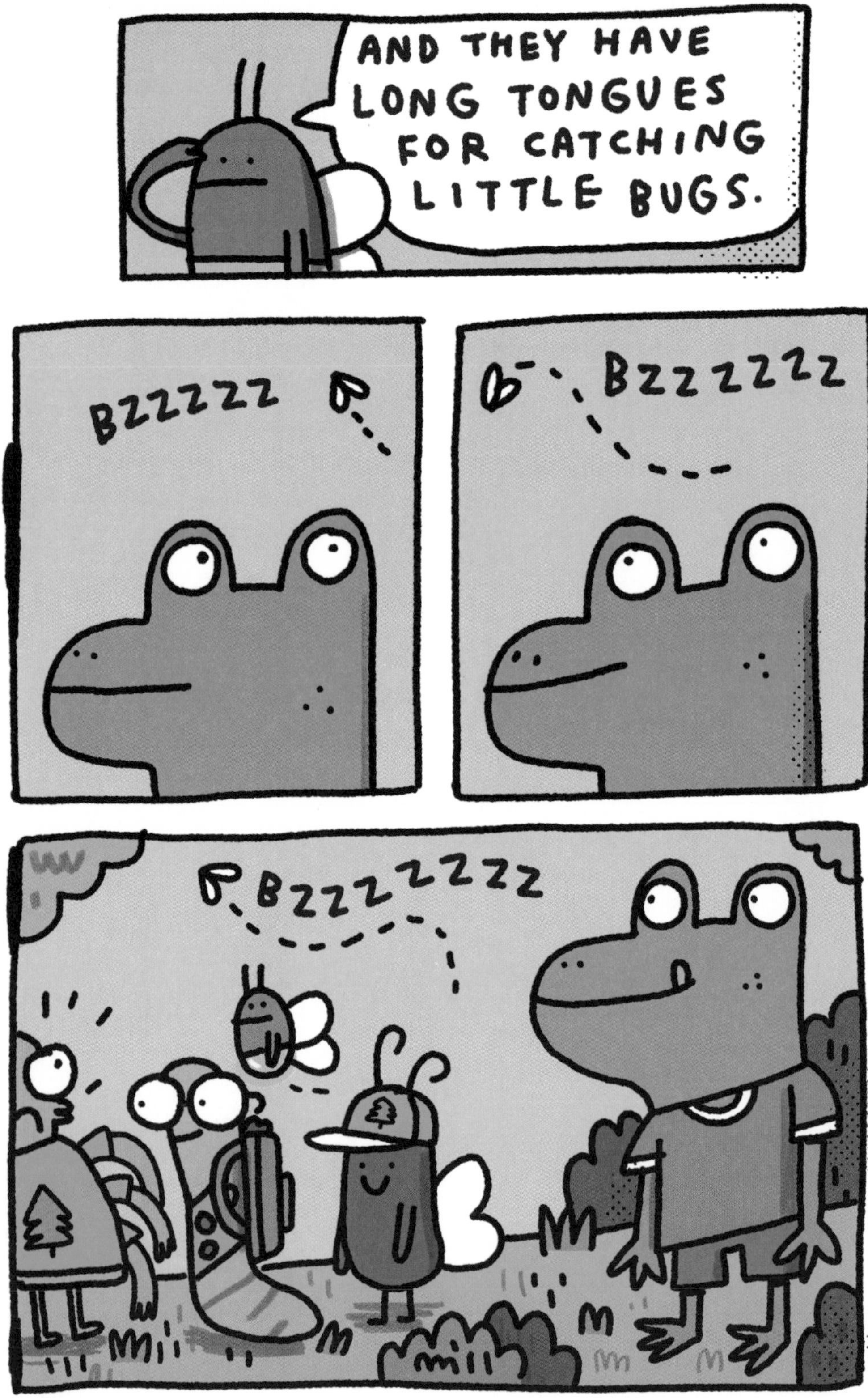
AND THEY HAVE LONG TONGUES FOR CATCHING LITTLE BUGS.
BZZZZZ
BZZZZZZZ
BZZZZZZZZ

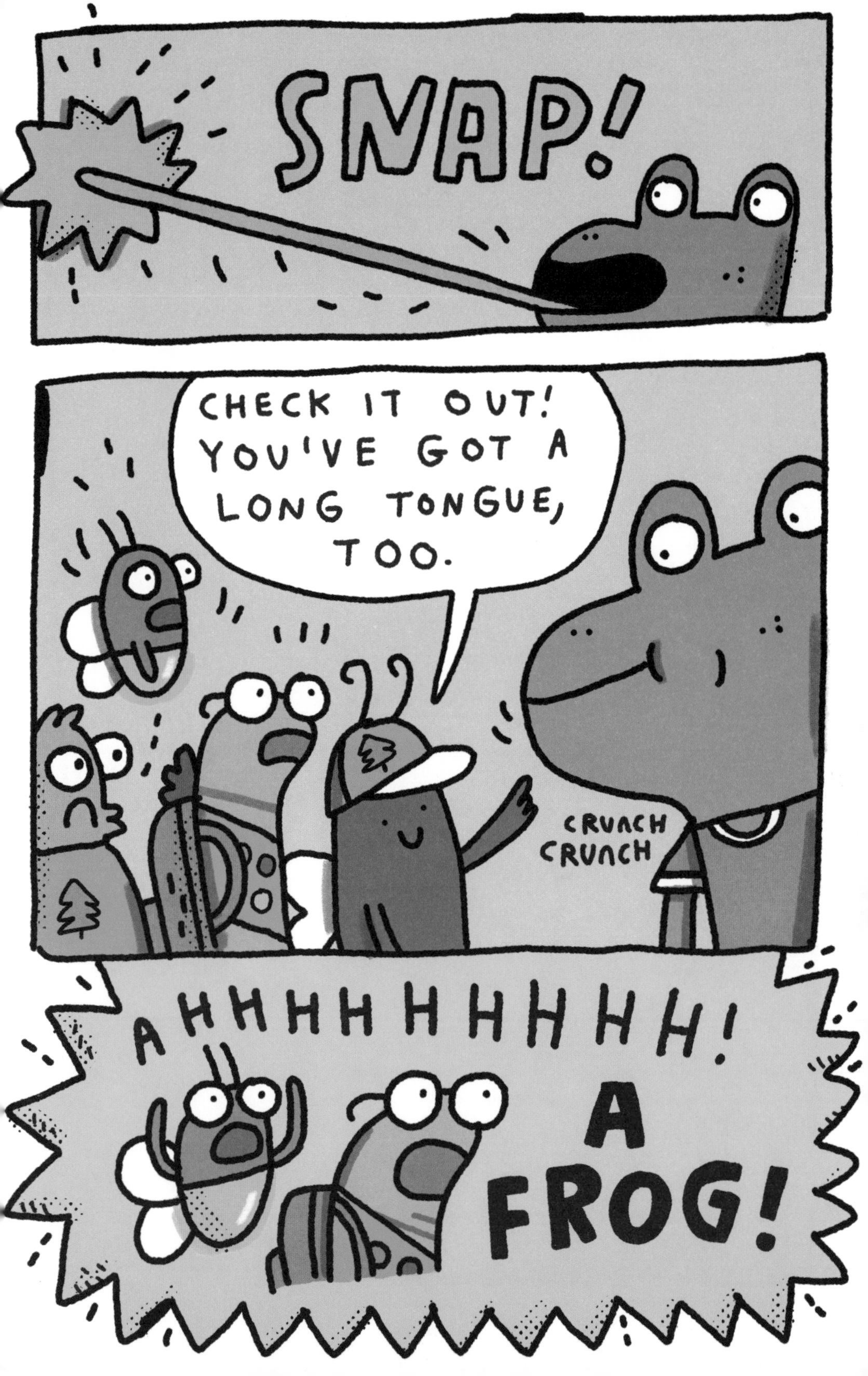
SNAP!
CHECK IT OUT! YOU'VE GOT A LONG TONGUE, TOO.
CRUNCH CRUNCH
AHHHHHHHHHH!
A FROG!

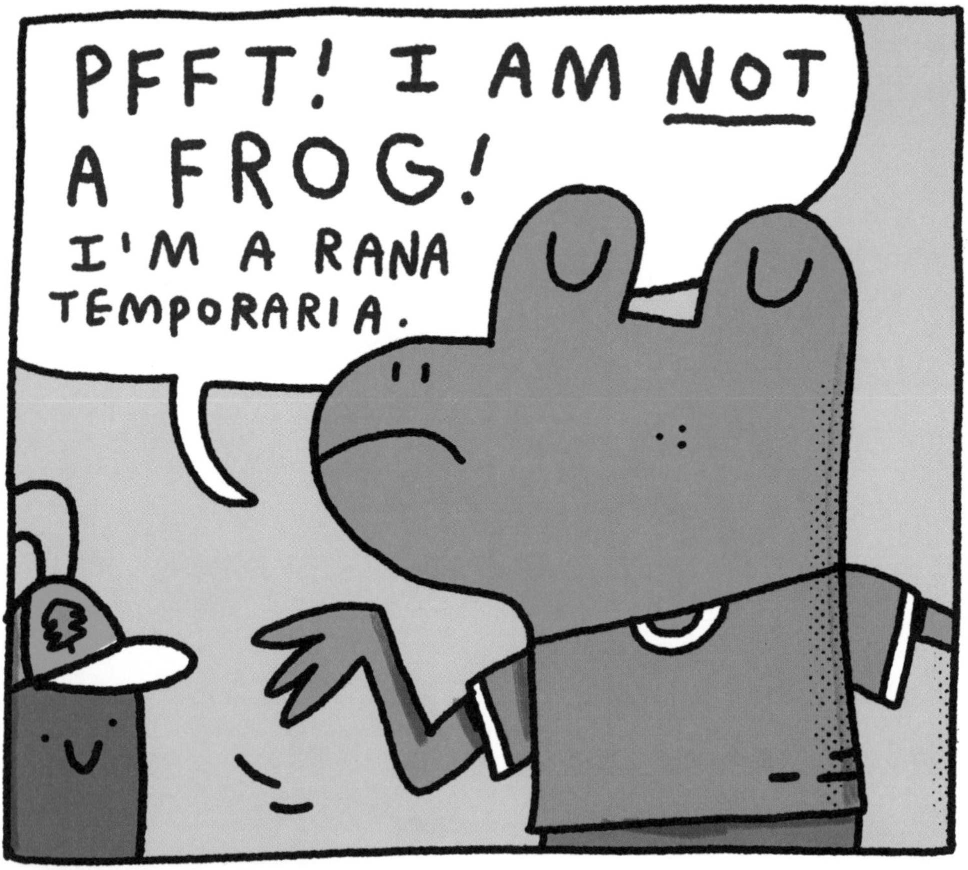
PFFT! I AM NOT A FROG!
I'M A RANA TEMPORARIA.

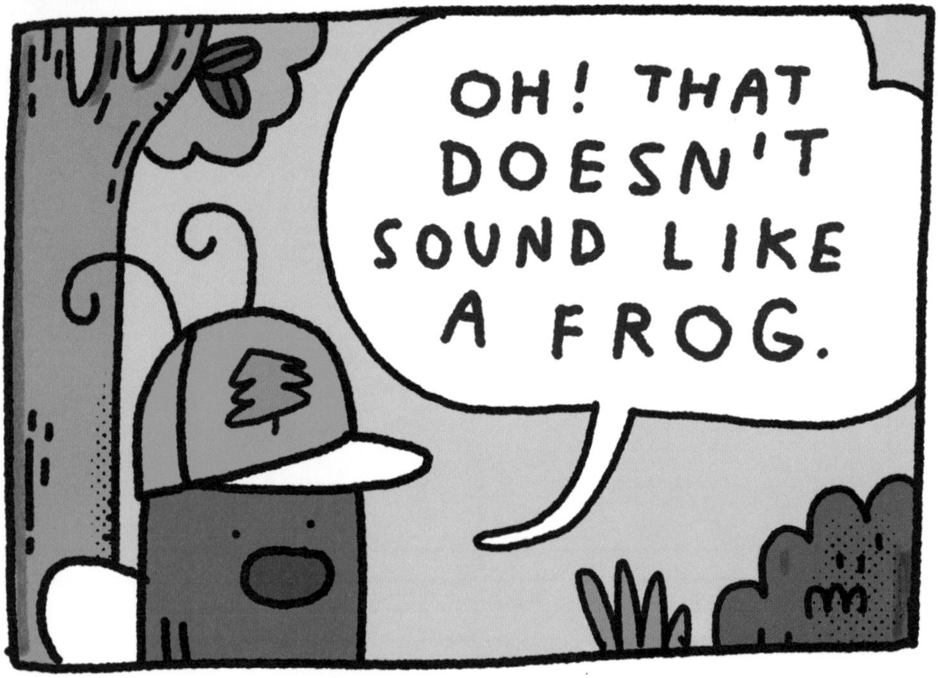
OH! THAT DOESN'T SOUND LIKE A FROG.

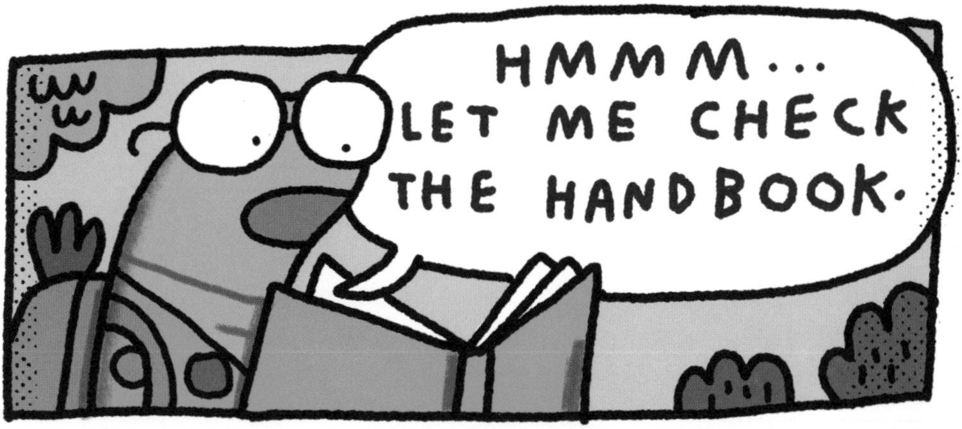
HMMM...
LET ME CHECK
THE HANDBOOK.

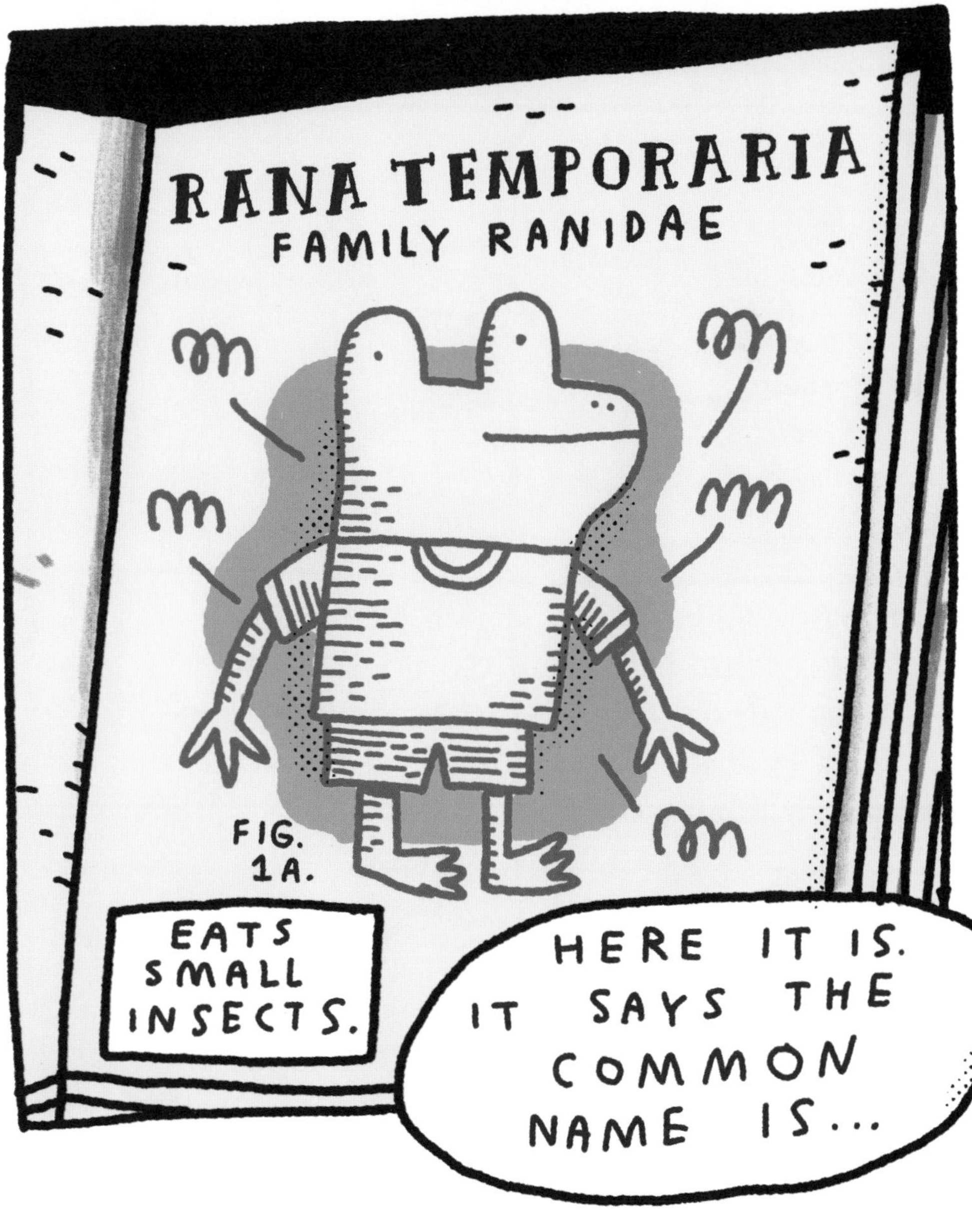
RANA TEMPORARIA
FAMILY RANIDAE
FIG.
1A.
EATS
SMALL
INSECTS.
HERE IT IS.
IT SAYS THE
COMMON
NAME IS...

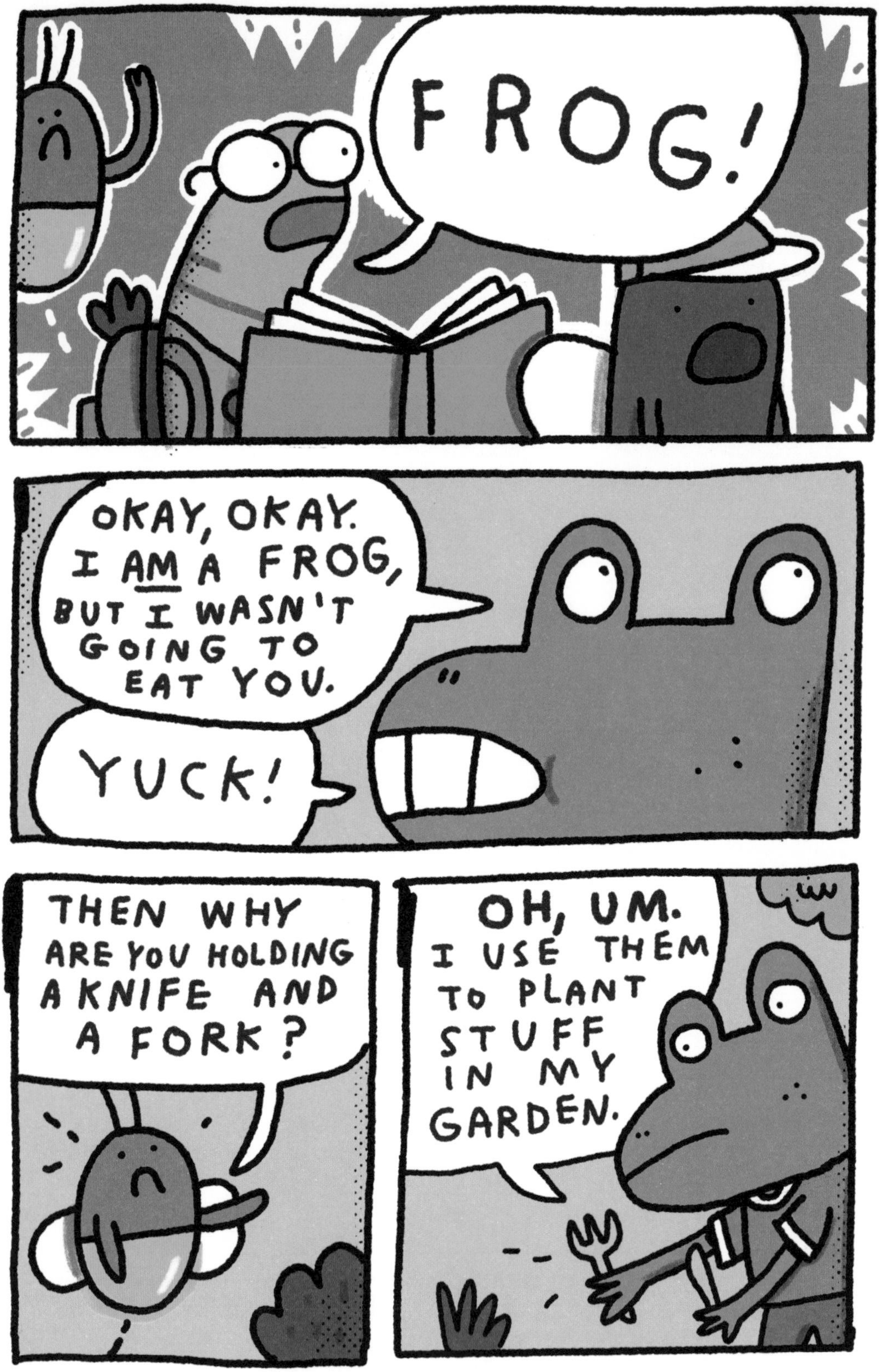
FROG!
OKAY, OKAY. I AM A FROG, BUT I WASN'T GOING TO EAT YOU.
YUCK!
THEN WHY ARE YOU HOLDING A KNIFE AND A FORK?
OH, UM. I USE THEM TO PLANT STUFF IN MY GARDEN.

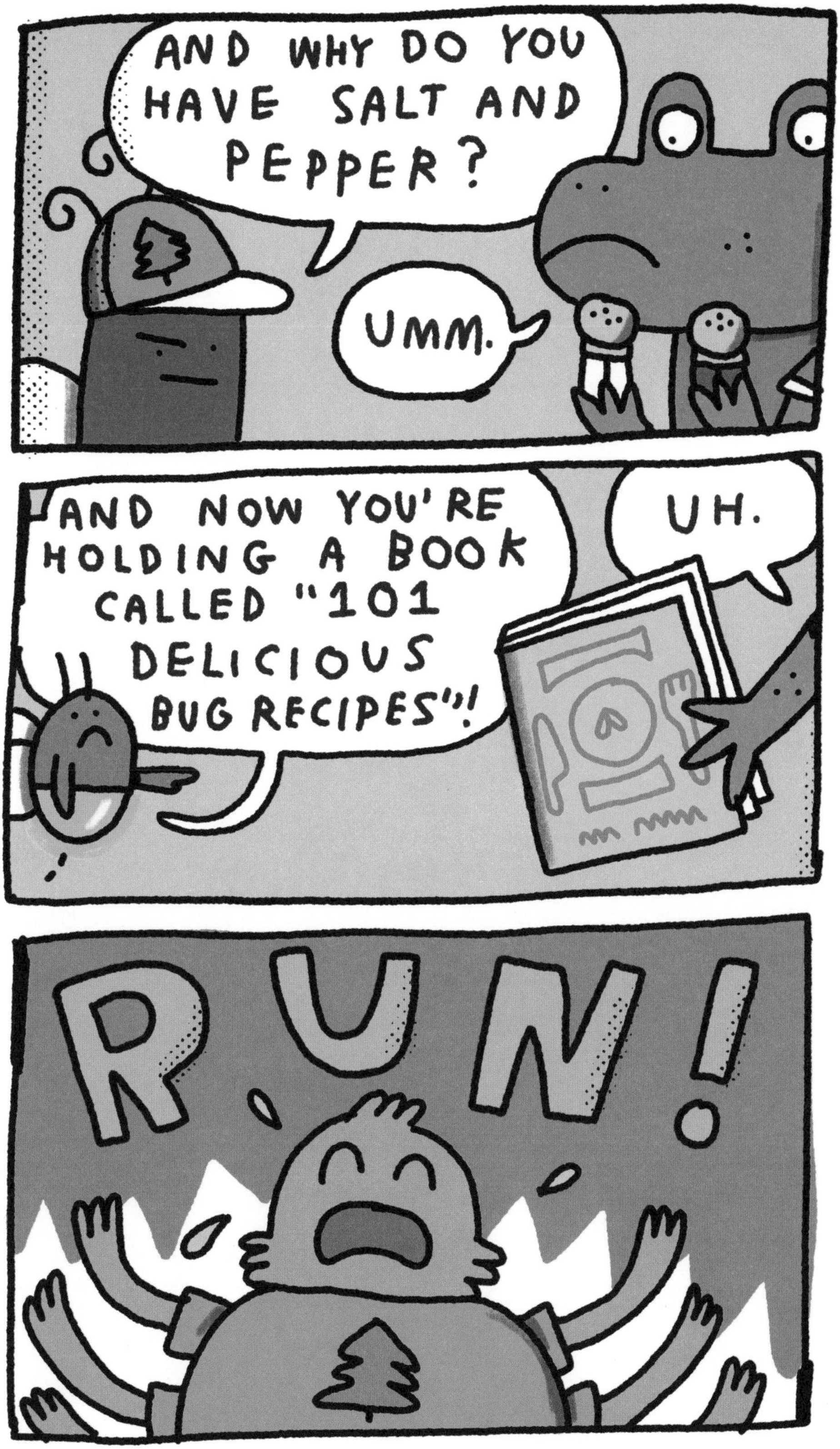
AND WHY DO YOU HAVE SALT AND PEPPER?
UMM.
AND NOW YOU'RE HOLDING A BOOK CALLED "101 DELICIOUS BUG RECIPES"!
UH.
RUN!

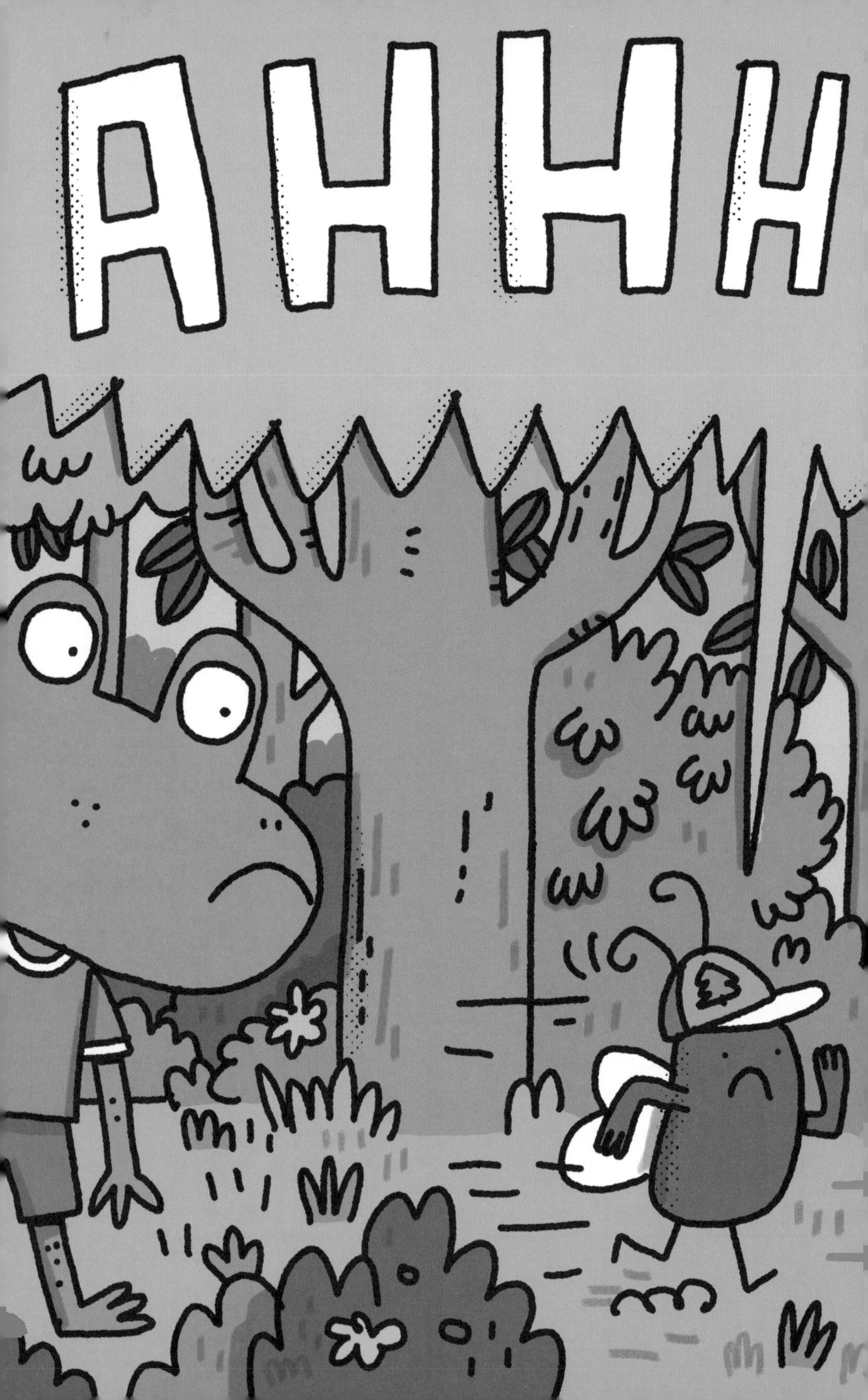
AHHH

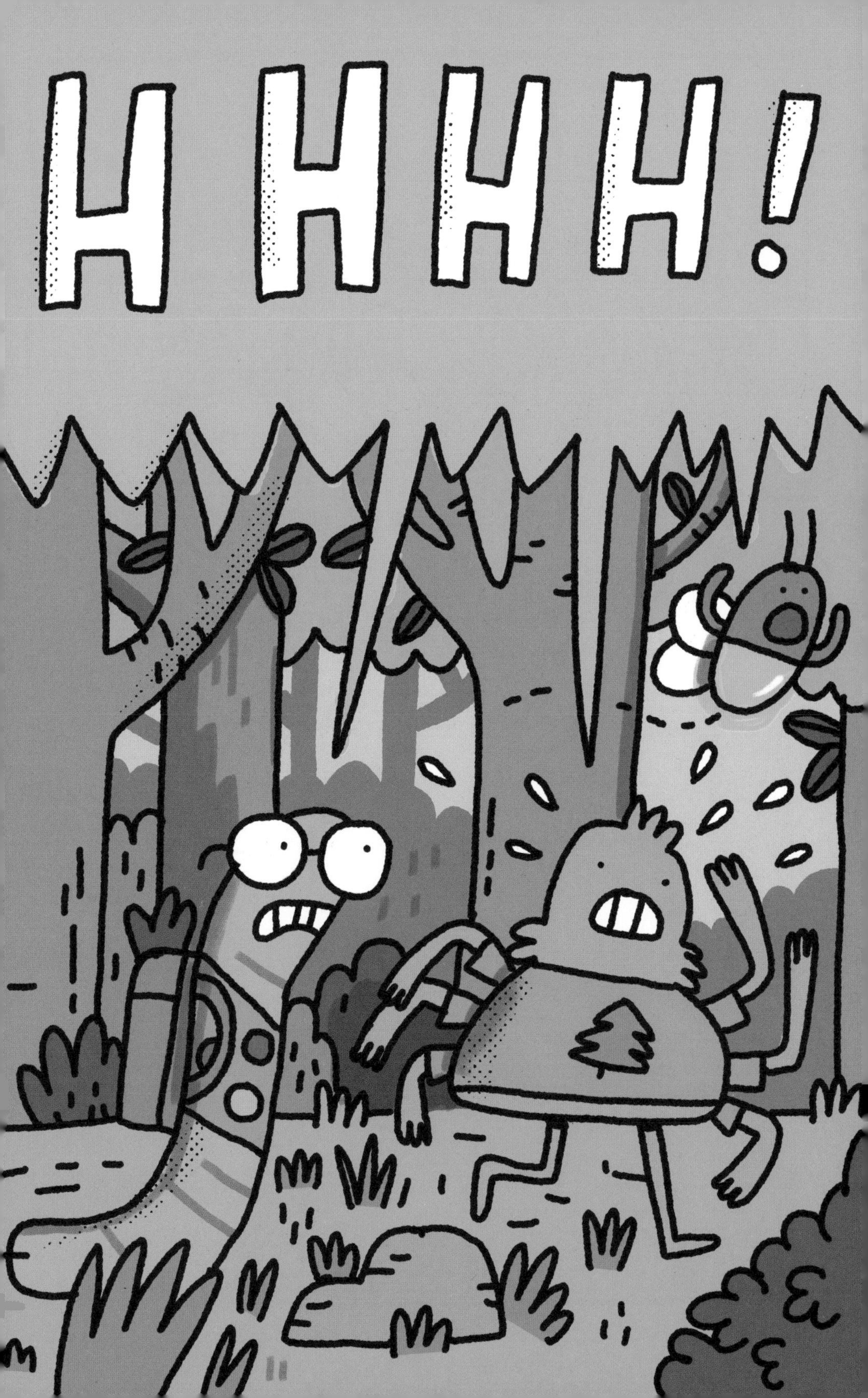
HHHH!

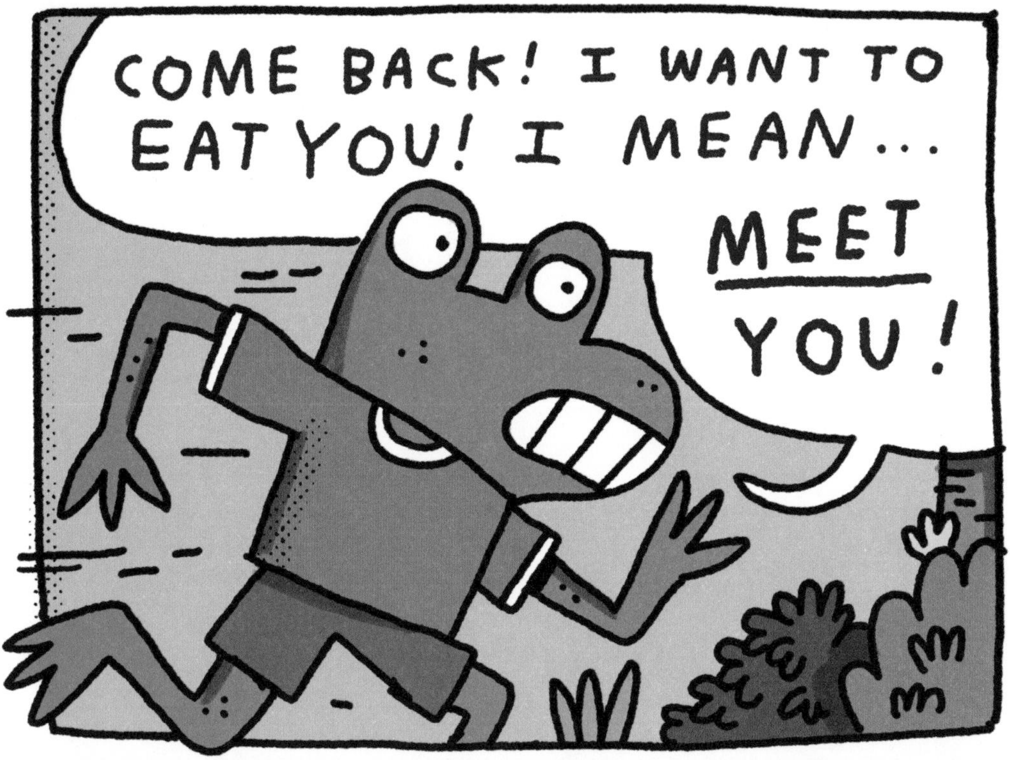
COME BACK! I WANT TO EAT YOU! I MEAN... MEET YOU!

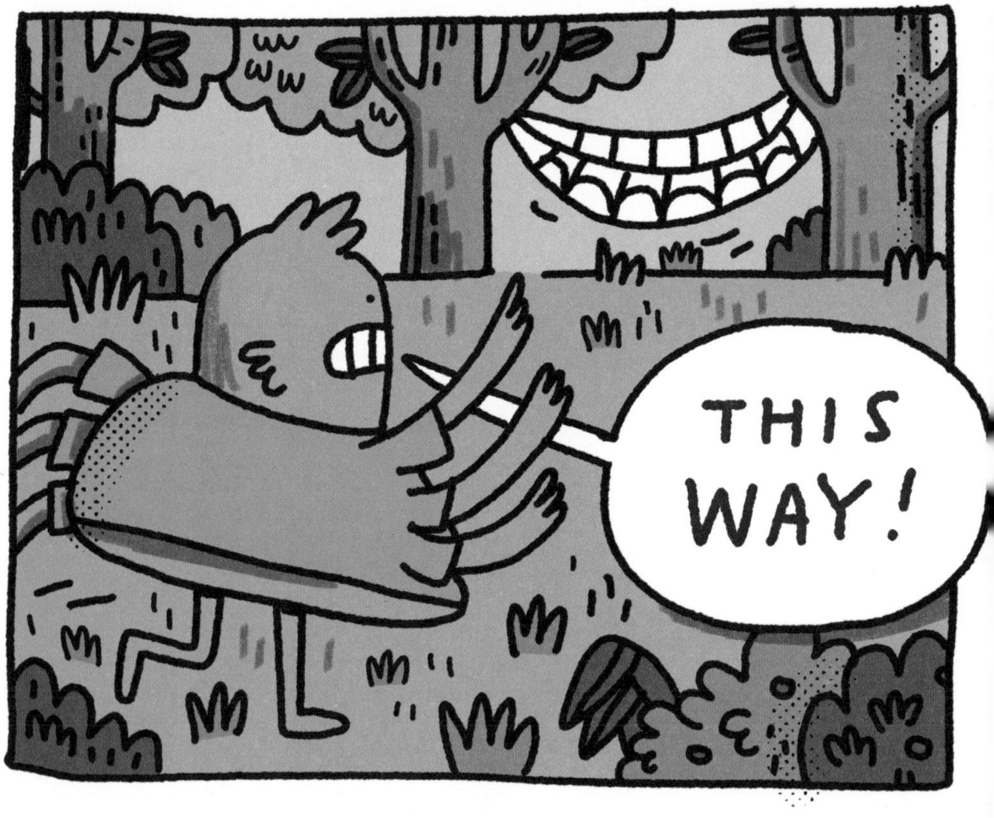
THIS WAY!

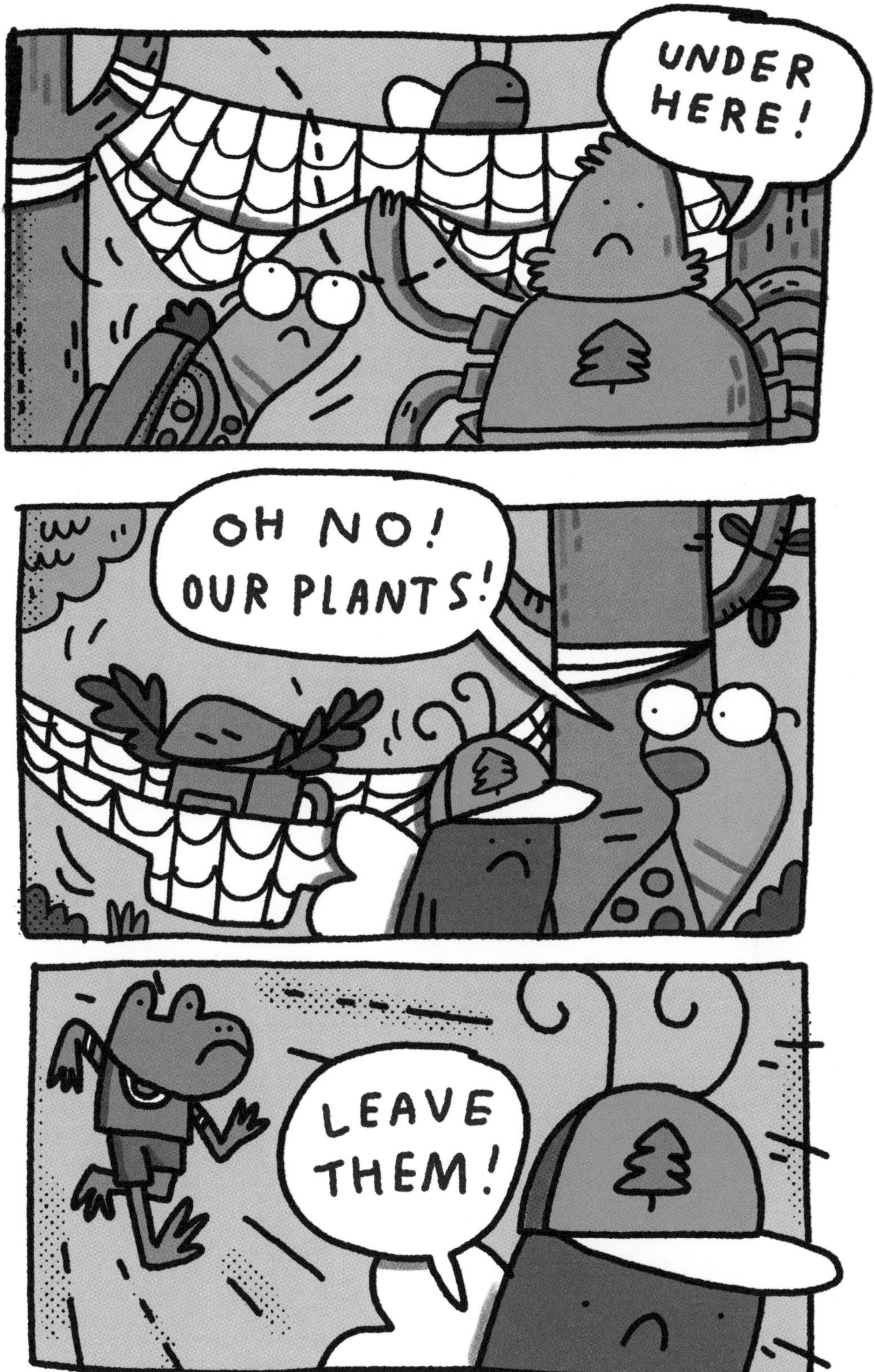
UNDER HERE!
OH NO! OUR PLANTS!
LEAVE THEM!

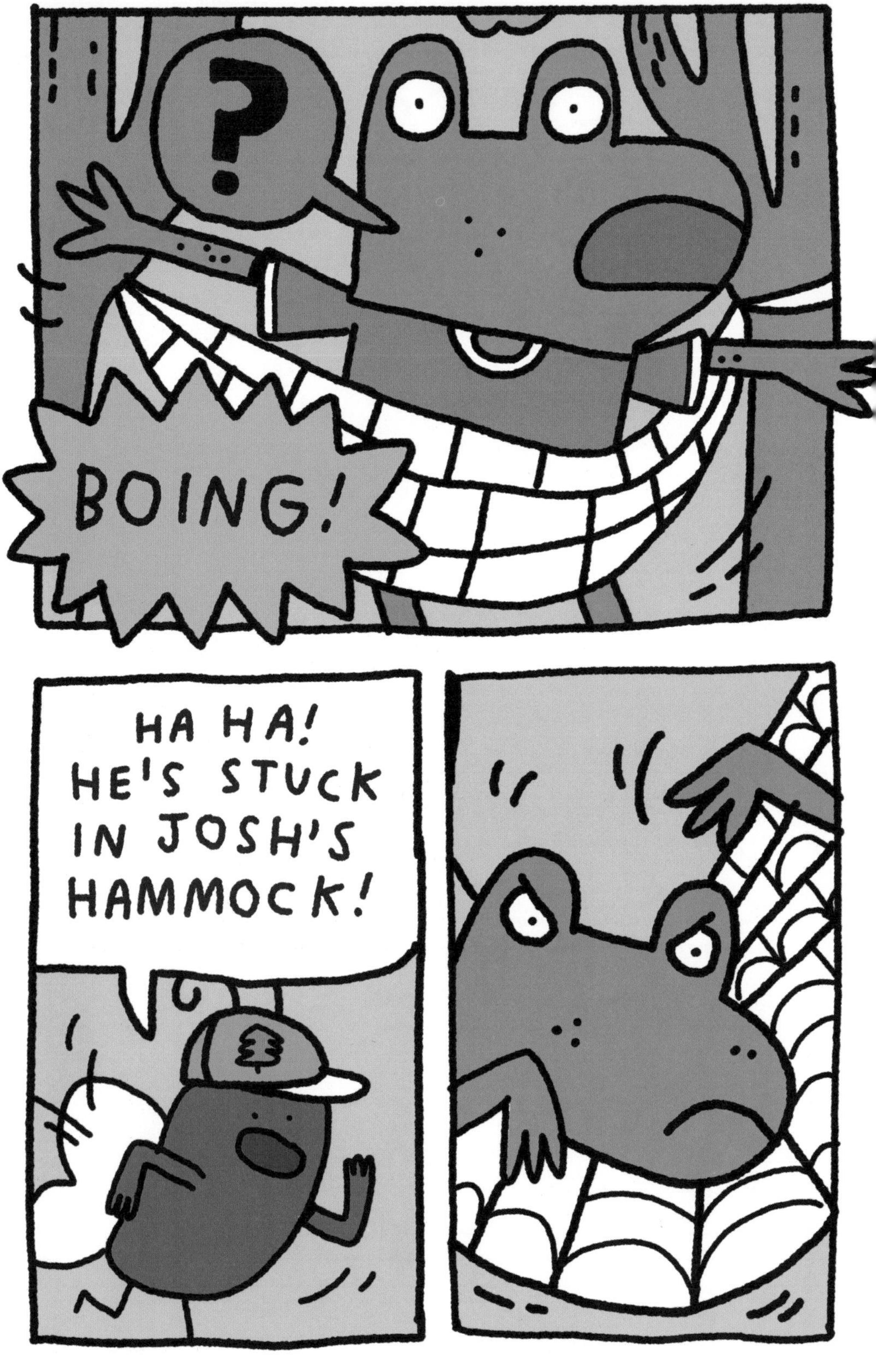
?
BOING!
HA HA! HE'S STUCK IN JOSH'S HAMMOCK!

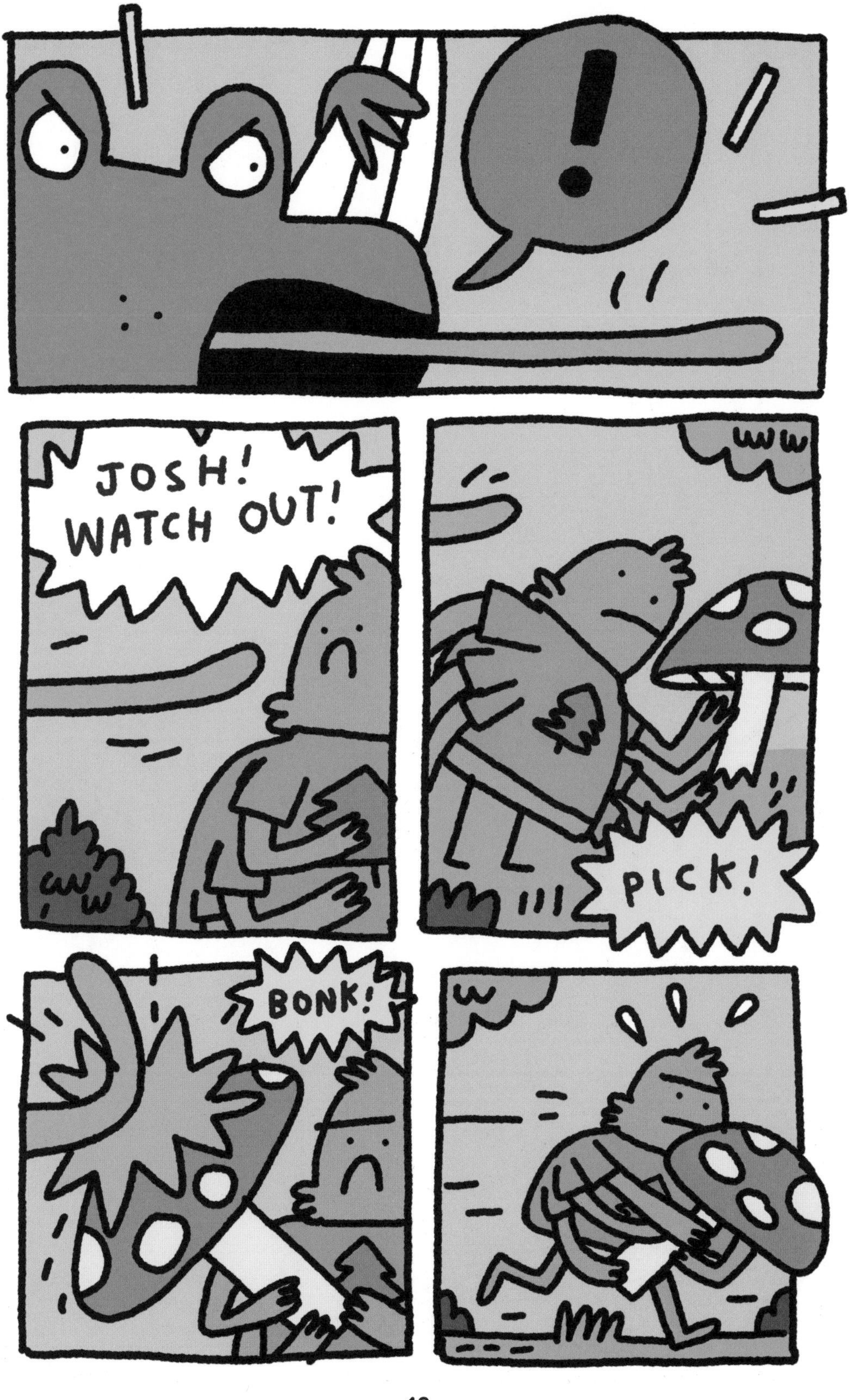
!
JOSH! WATCH OUT!
PICK!
BONK!

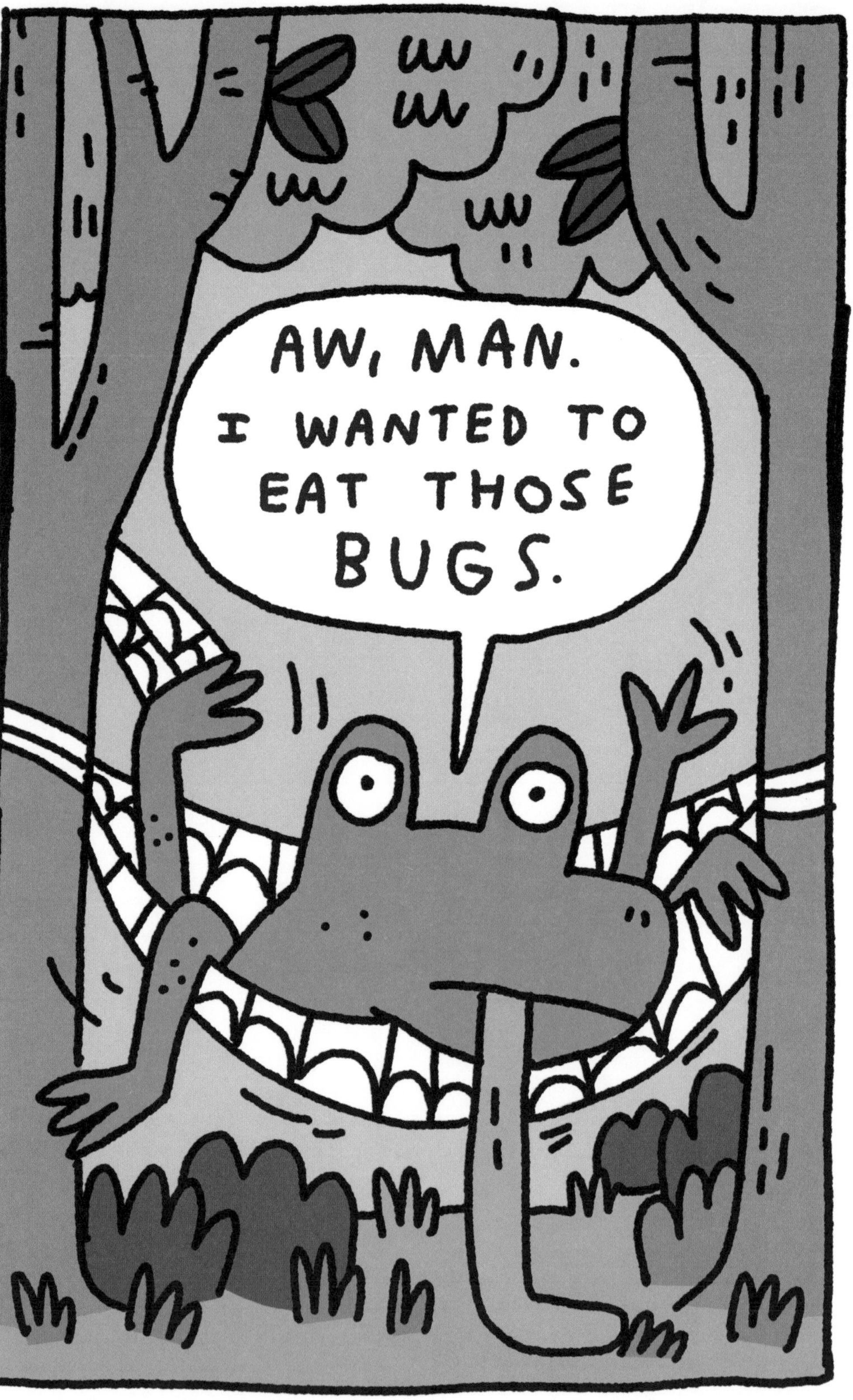
AW, MAN. I WANTED TO EAT THOSE BUGS.

CHAPTER 5

BACK AT

HEADQUARTERS

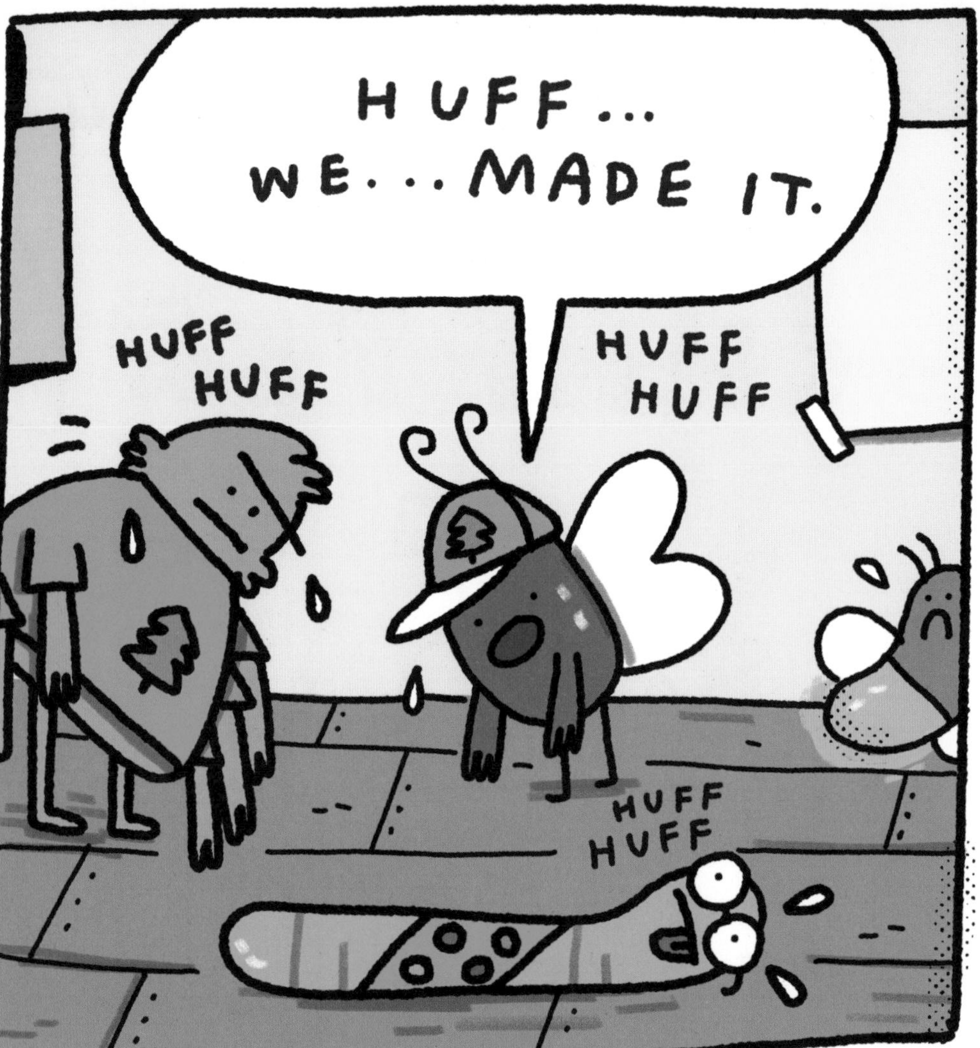
HUFF... WE...MADE IT.
HUFF HUFF
HUFF HUFF
HUFF HUFF

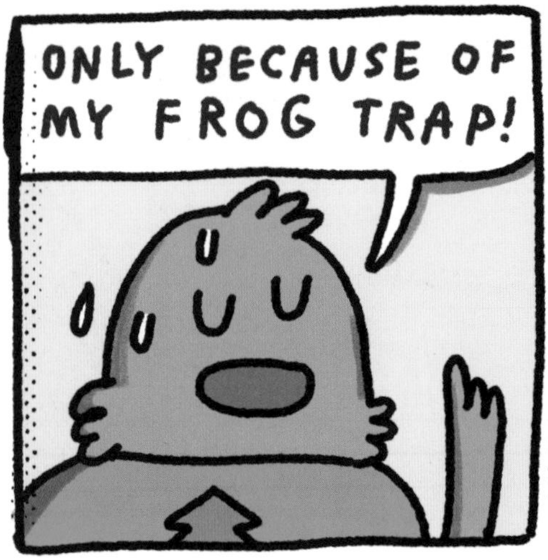
ONLY BECAUSE OF MY FROG TRAP!

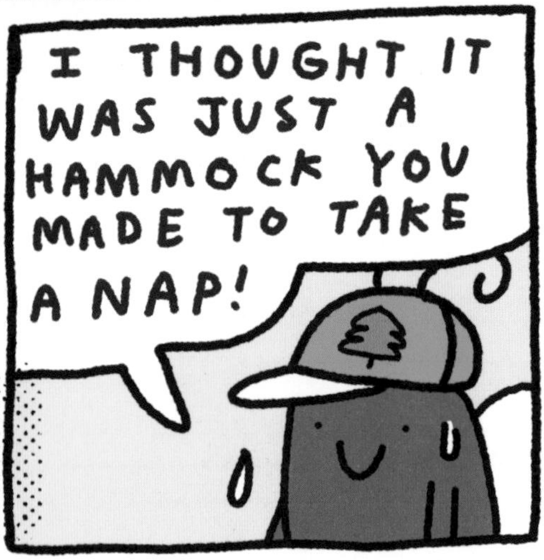
I THOUGHT IT WAS JUST A HAMMOCK YOU MADE TO TAKE A NAP!

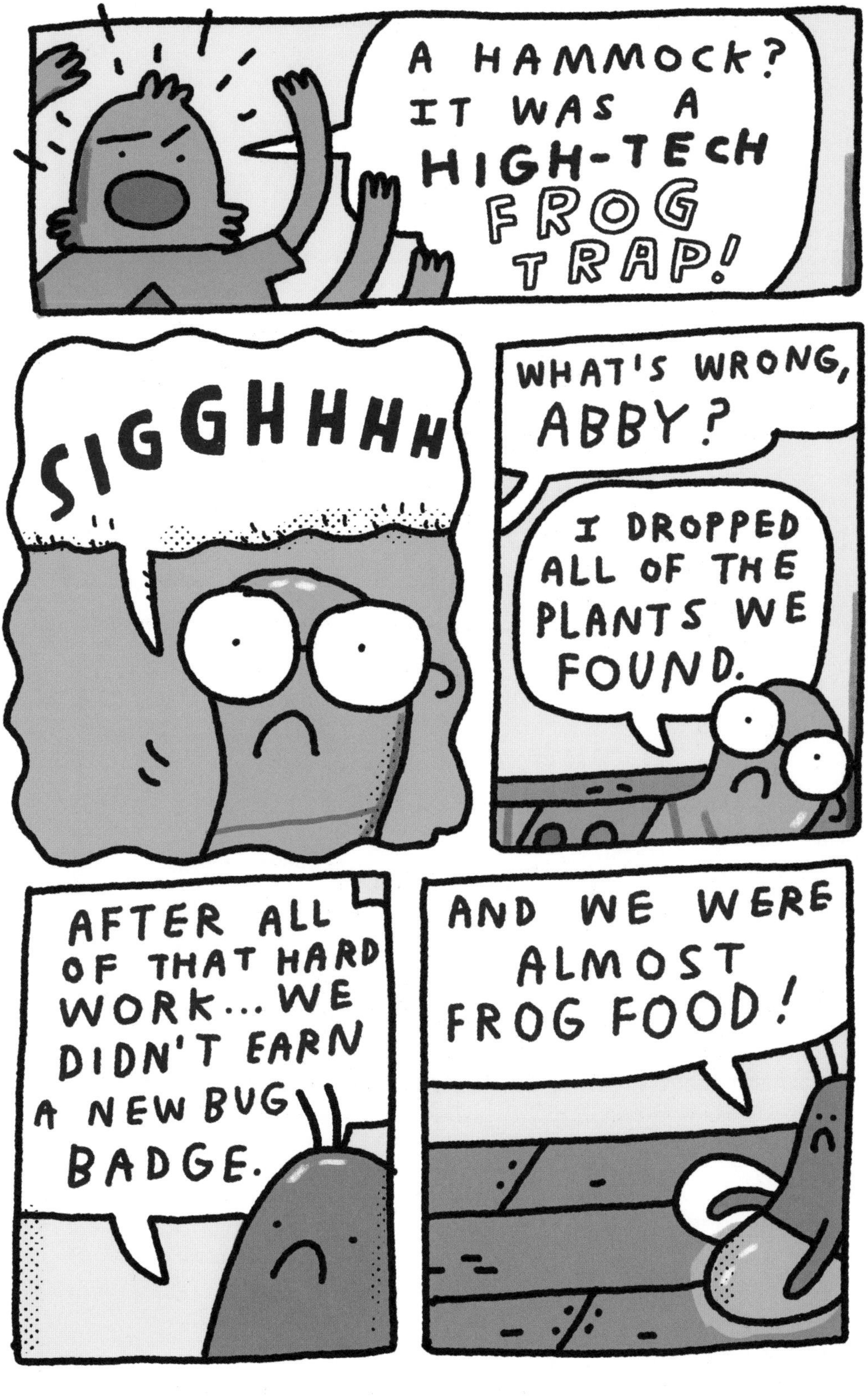
A HAMMOCK? IT WAS A HIGH-TECH FROG TRAP!
SIGGHHHH
WHAT'S WRONG, ABBY?
I DROPPED ALL OF THE PLANTS WE FOUND.
AFTER ALL OF THAT HARD WORK... WE DIDN'T EARN A NEW BUG BADGE.
AND WE WERE ALMOST FROG FOOD!

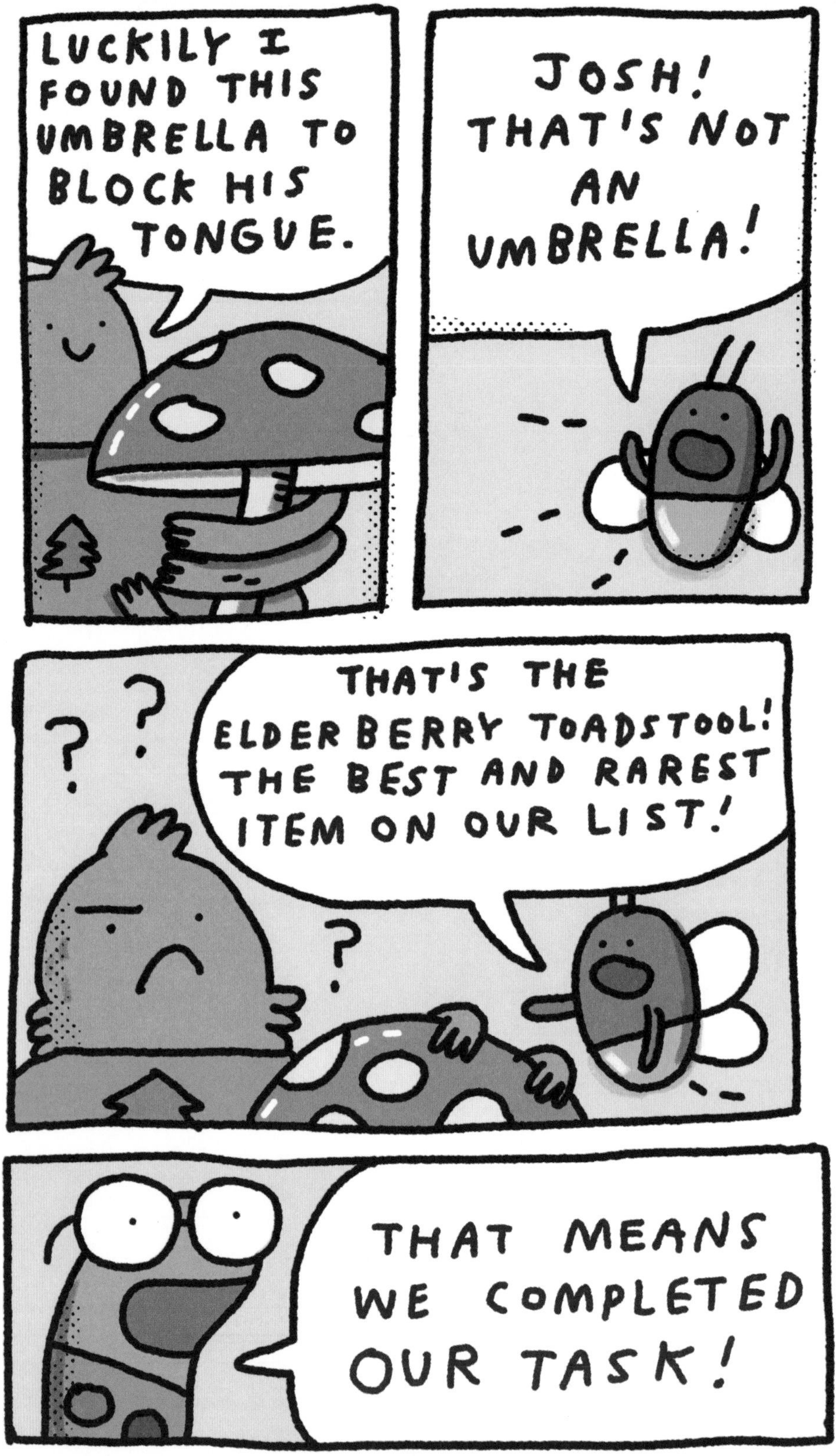
LUCKILY I FOUND THIS UMBRELLA TO BLOCK HIS TONGUE.
JOSH! THAT'S NOT AN UMBRELLA!
THAT'S THE ELDERBERRY TOADSTOOL! THE BEST AND RAREST ITEM ON OUR LIST!
THAT MEANS WE COMPLETED OUR TASK!

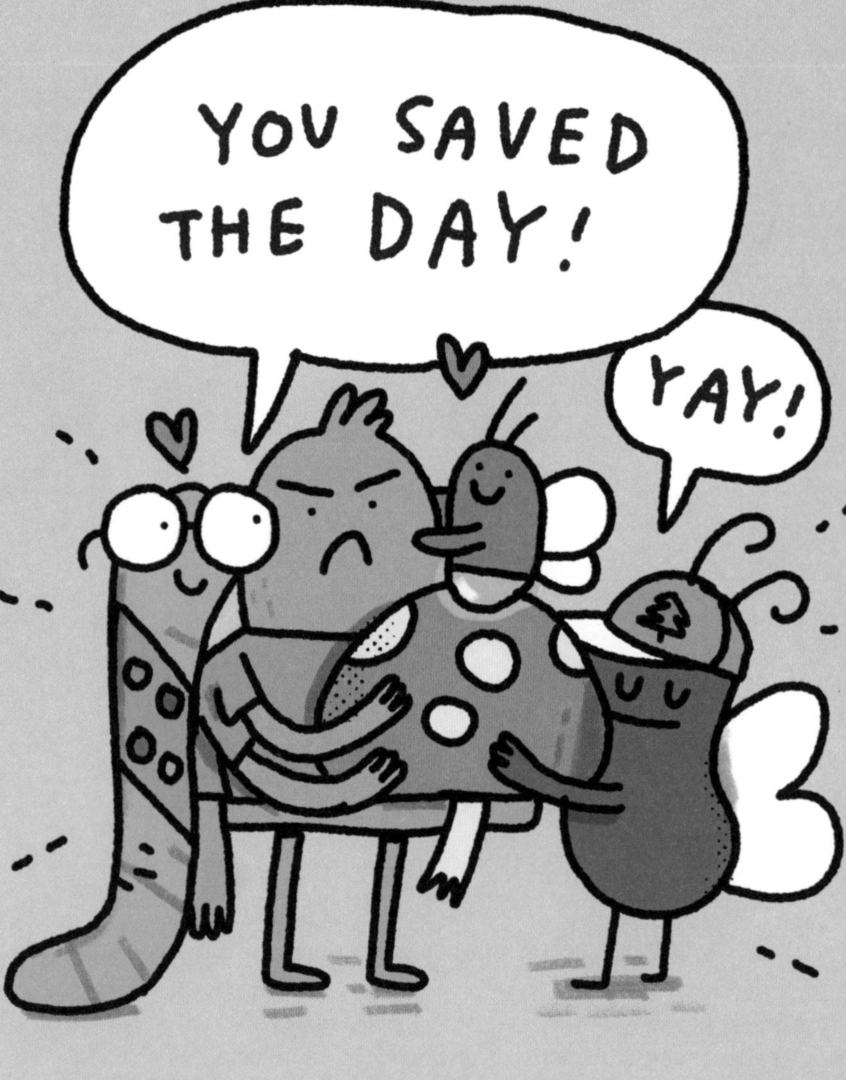
YOU SAVED THE DAY!
YAY!

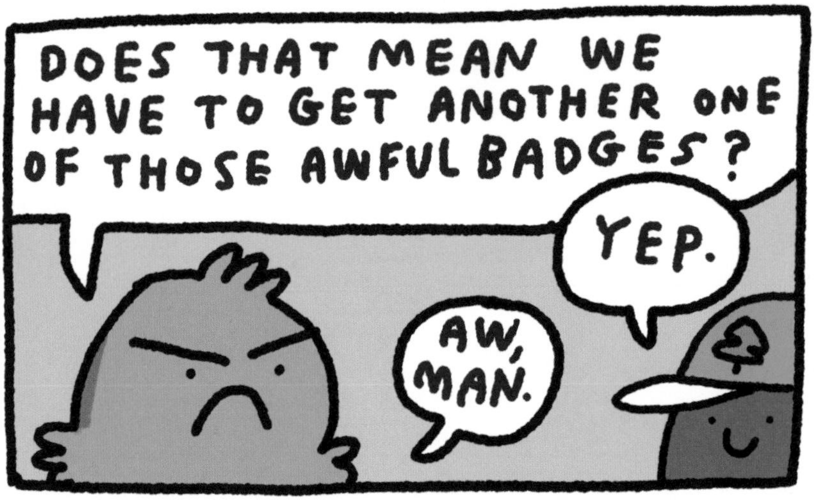
DOES THAT MEAN WE HAVE TO GET ANOTHER ONE OF THOSE AWFUL BADGES?
YEP.
AW, MAN.

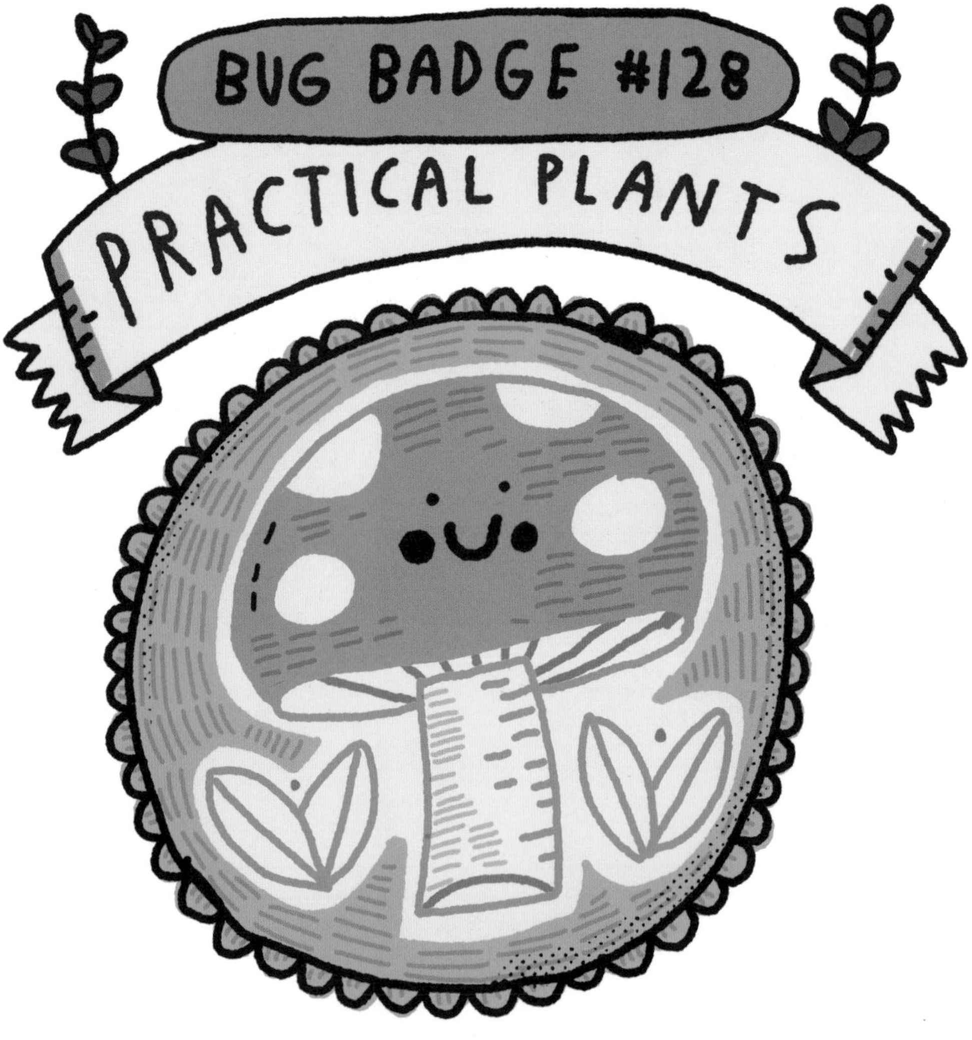
BUG BADGE #128
PRACTICAL PLANTS

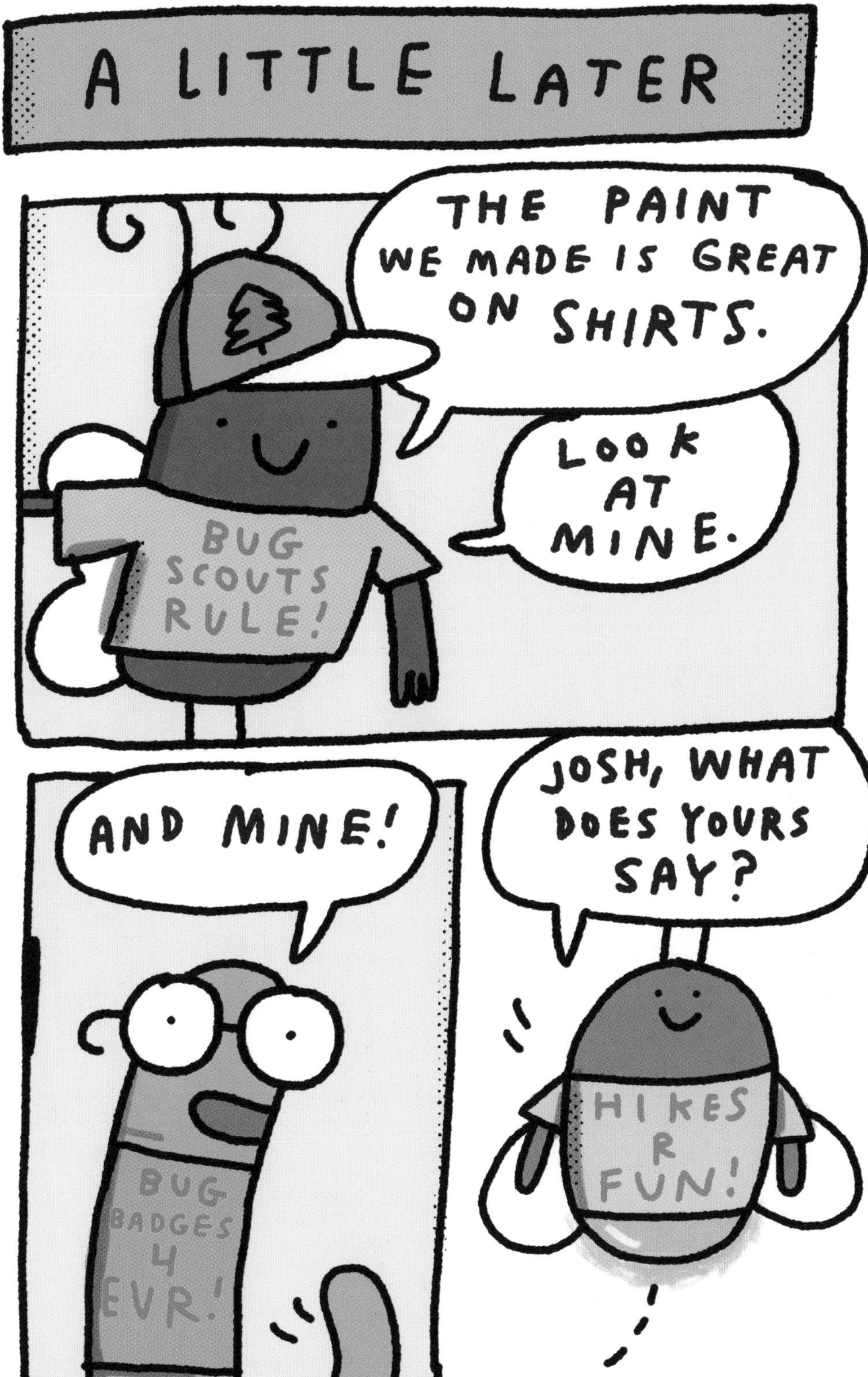
A LITTLE LATER
THE PAINT WE MADE IS GREAT ON SHIRTS.
LOOK AT MINE.
BUG SCOUTS RULE!
AND MINE!
JOSH, WHAT DOES YOURS SAY?
BUG BADGES 4 EVR!
HIKES R FUN!

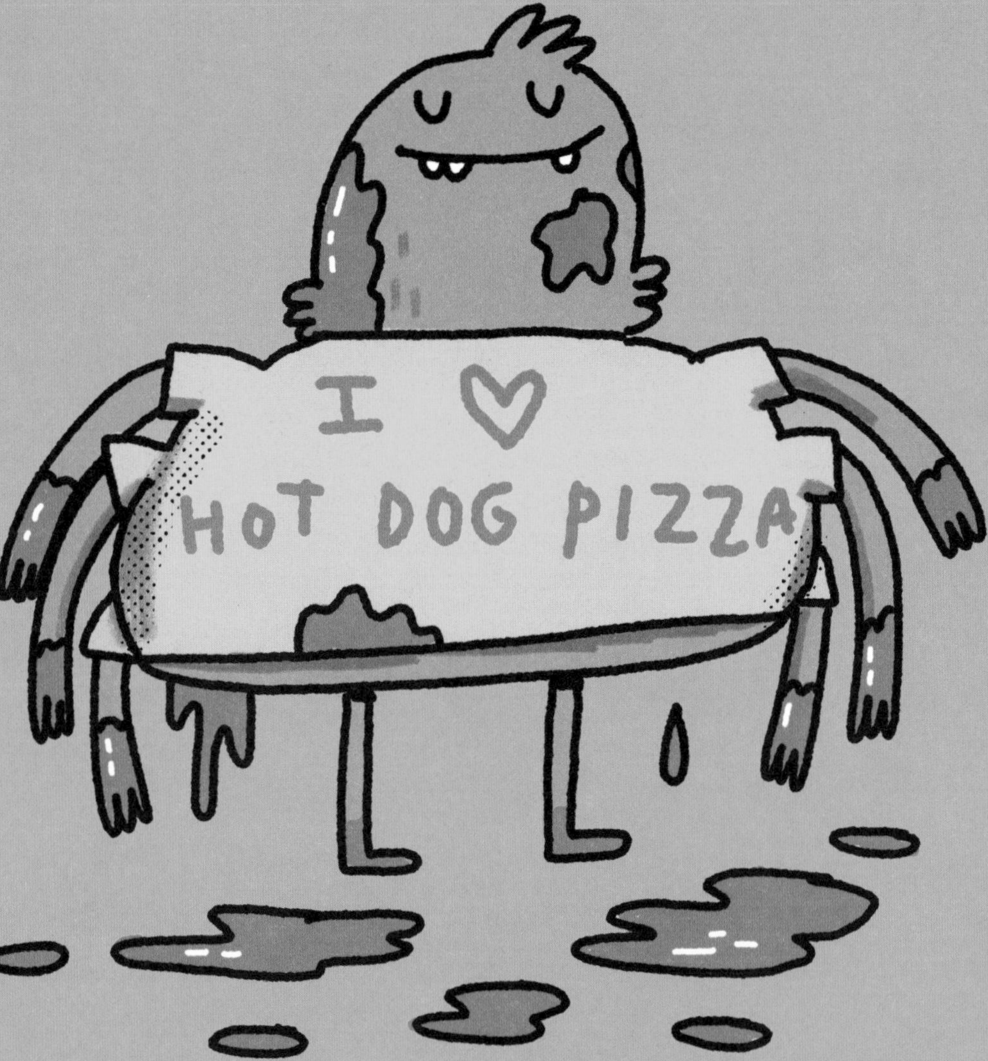
I ♡
HOT DOG PIZZA

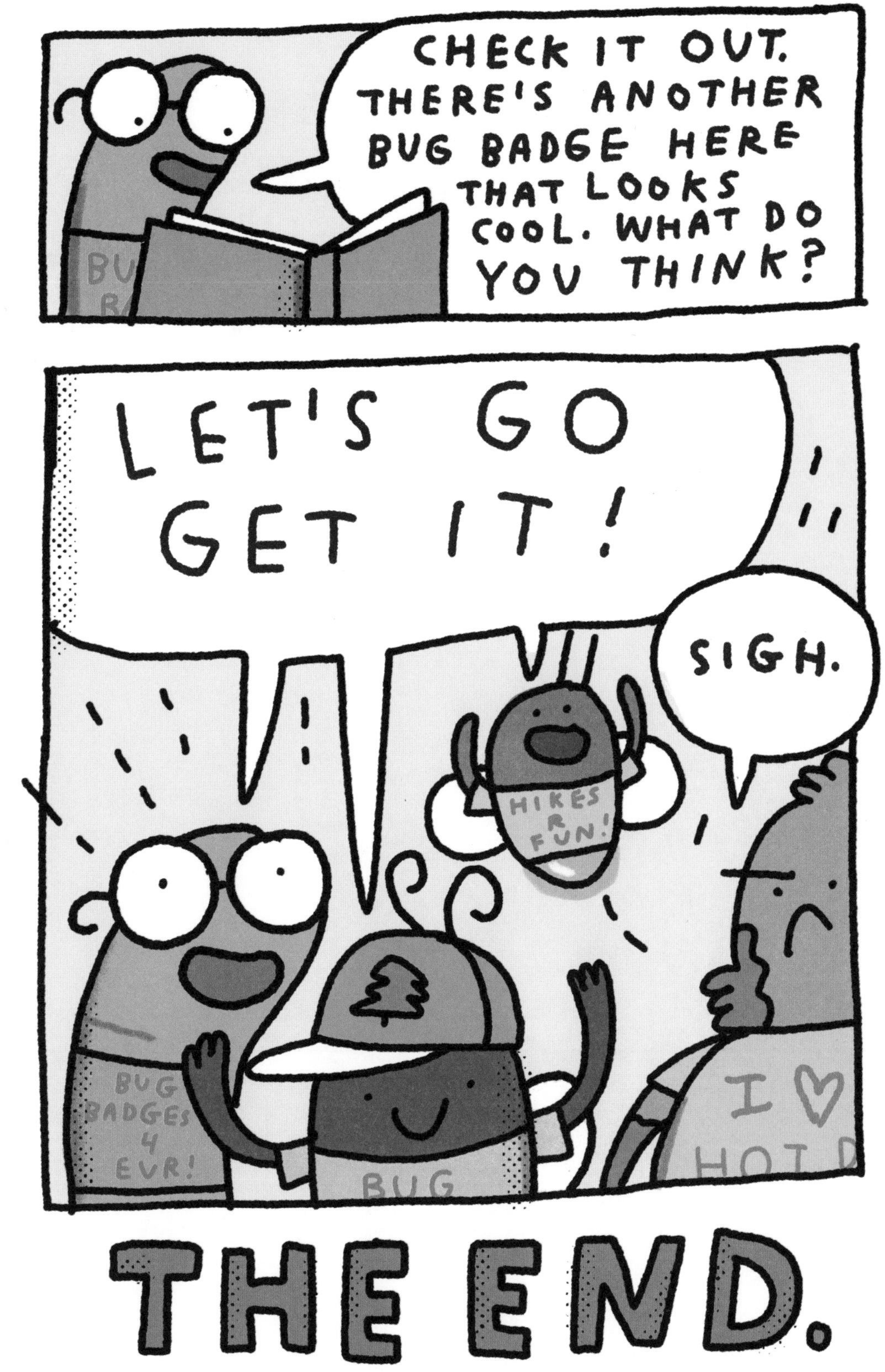
CHECK IT OUT. THERE'S ANOTHER BUG BADGE HERE THAT LOOKS COOL. WHAT DO YOU THINK?
LET'S GO GET IT!
SIGH.
HIKES R FUN!
BUG BADGES 4 EVR!
BUG

THE END.

MIKE LOWERY

is the illustrator of many books for kids, including the *New York Times* bestselling Mac B., Kid Spy books. He is also the creator of the Everything Awesome books. He lives in Atlanta with his amazing wife and super-genius kids. He collects weird facts and draws them every day in his sketchbook. See them on Instagram at: @mikelowerystudio.